A Dash of Murder

A Myrtle Clover Cozy Mystery, Volume 19

Elizabeth Craig

Published by Elizabeth Spann Craig, 2022.

This is a work of fiction. Similarities to real people, places, or events are entirely coincidental.

A DASH OF MURDER

First edition. January 20, 2022.

Copyright © 2022 Elizabeth Craig.

Written by Elizabeth Craig.

Chapter One

"The Bradley Museum is hosting free tours today," offered Miles, reading from a website on his phone. "Apparently, there are to be 'hands-on activities.'"

"Been there, done that," said Myrtle. "I was a docent at the museum, remember? I can give that spiel in my sleep."

"Not that you would know, given how very little you sleep."

"It seems to me, Miles, that you're unfamiliar with the concept of sleeping, yourself," said Myrtle with dignity. "After all, we're both currently sitting out on my dock alongside my feral cat, watching the water and eating ice cream at three o'clock in the morning."

Pasha, the feral cat in question, blinked at them as the dock gently bobbed.

The truth of this remark made Miles sigh. "Well, at least we're able to enjoy being outdoors."

"Exactly. I couldn't stand another minute inside, but the only time being outdoors is tolerable is in the middle of the night. I'm surprised more people aren't doing outside activities right now. The football players at the high school should be practicing now. You know how late teens stay up. This would be the ideal time for football practice."

Miles said wryly, "I doubt the coaches would agree, considering they're not in their teens anymore."

"Well, in the middle of an October heatwave, it would behoove them to rethink their antipathy to nocturnal practices." Myrtle sniffed.

Miles resumed looking for local indoor activities on his phone. "The Women's Club is hosting bingo tomorrow."

"Pass."

"It's for charity," said Miles.

Myrtle sighed. "That means we'll have to pay admission to go in. My budget is a little constrained this week. And I'm planning for us to go to the diner at least once."

Miles raised his eyebrows. "Are you? I didn't know dining out was part of the plan."

"Well, I figured it would get us out of our houses and into another air-conditioned building. We'll just have to drive over there since it's too hot to walk." Myrtle scowled at the lake. "It's a pity we old folks don't really perspire anymore. My younger self wouldn't think these temperatures were all that hot."

"I don't think you're giving your younger self enough credit. This type of heat is recognizable by anyone, perspiring or not."

Myrtle said, "I suppose so. It's just frustrating. Even worse, Red called me up yesterday evening and told me he wanted to have a conversation with me later this morning."

"That sounds ominous," said Miles. "Usually he just comes over without prior notification."

"Exactly. He lives directly across the street, after all. Scheduling a talk makes it sound as if he's going to insert himself in my business once again." Myrtle's face darkened at the thought.

"Maybe he won't this time. Maybe he needs to talk with you about Elaine's birthday or something."

"Elaine's birthday is months away," said Myrtle gloomily.

"Can you think what he might be wanting to speak with you about?"

Myrtle made a face. "I've been mulling over all the unsavory possibilities. He might be wanting to do a safety inspection—that's a favorite of his."

"Oh, like checking the smoke detectors and whatnot?"

Myrtle said, "It goes far beyond smoke detectors. He inspects my throw rugs to make sure they're firmly taped to the floor. He makes sure there aren't any slipping hazards in the bathroom. And he takes special care over the oven."

Miles wisely didn't comment on the oven. The poor appliance had seen its share of culinary calamities. "Is there anything else he might be wanting to talk about?"

"There's always Red's usual pitch for sending me to the Greener Pastures Retirement Home. He hasn't tried that one in the last month or so. However, it would be unusual for him to focus an entire visit on it. He's much more likely to slip the virtues of the retirement home into casual conversation. Red always believes he's being so subtle: 'Mama, I know Puddin is getting on your nerves. If you went to Greener Pastures, you'd have housekeeping service every day. And *cheerful* housekeepers.' Or: 'Mama, don't you look forward to the days when you don't have to worry about yardwork? Or Dusty even showing up to do it? That's one of the nice things about Greener Pastures.'"

Miles swallowed a bit of his ice cream and said thoughtfully, "That doesn't sound very subtle to me."

"Nor me. It's just Red's idea of subtlety. I suppose his career as a police chief hasn't prepared him well for nuance." She paused. "He could be coming by to complain about Elaine's new hobby. He realizes we're allies when hobbies are involved."

Miles shook his head. "That poor woman."

"Yes. There are many areas Elaine excels in, but she unerringly pursues things she's inept at."

"What's the hobby du jour?" asked Miles.

"I haven't asked, although I'm certain I'll find out soon. It's about the time she'd try one again."

Miles said thoughtfully, "You know, in some ways it's sort of a hopeful gesture, isn't it? The persistence of mankind's faith and endurance in the face of failure?"

"Is it? I suppose it could be, if you're determined to take an optimistic point of view toward it."

Miles said, "Going back to the problem of acceptable activities, don't you have garden club coming up? That's something you can do that you usually enjoy."

"Well, that's true, although it's fairly ironic that we would *talk* about doing outside work but then not be able to *do* it because of the heat. The nice thing is that Tippy is hosting it and she always does a nice job. She'll have wonderful hors d'oeuvres and the program will run like a well-oiled machine. Unlike Erma's ghastly stab at hosting last month." Myrtle shuddered. Erma was her obnoxious next-door neighbor. She avoided her as much as possible, but encounters *would* happen on Myrtle's worst days.

"Book club should be coming up relatively soon, too," offered Miles. He jumped as Pasha suddenly decided to leap into his lap.

Myrtle chuckled. "Sweet Pasha! She's trying to be friends."

Miles wasn't at all sure that was Pasha's intention. She peered intently into his face, seemingly interested by the glasses he wore. He pushed them up his nose nervously and Pasha watched with unblinking interest.

Myrtle added, "Book club won't be coming up for a couple of weeks. I have yet to decide if I'm going to try to skim the insipid content of this particular pick. I'm not sure what Blanche was thinking when she chose this book. I'll assume she was in a tremendous hurry and grabbed the first novel she found at the library. The club would do a lot better if the members actually asked a librarian what they recommend."

"Have you come up with a good idea for your pick?" asked Miles. "You're not going to try to get anyone to read something too onerous again, are you?"

"This is a group that struggles with *The Outsiders*, so no. I'm toying with the idea of introducing them to some of the children's classics for the next time I need to pick. Maybe *Rebecca of Sunnybrook Farm* or *Little Women* or something."

Miles carefully drew his head back a little from Pasha's probing gaze. Pasha, in turn, leaned forward a little, her tail swishing just a bit.

"Myrtle, I'm thinking it's time I went inside and tried to sleep again. Pasha appears to have some sort of fixation with my glasses or my nose or something. I have the terrible feeling she's going to leap at my face and bite it."

"The little darling! She's so implacable, isn't she? Sphinx-like. But you never know what a feral animal might do next. They're absolutely fascinating."

"And worrisome," said Miles. "Can you help extricate me? I'm not sure I can move right now and I don't want to startle her."

"You most certainly *shouldn't* startle her, Miles. That would be a very bad decision."

Myrtle gently leaned to the side and cooed at Pasha until the black cat ceased her examination of Miles and looked inquisitively at Myrtle. Myrtle reached out her hand and Pasha lovingly rubbed her head against it.

Miles gave a sigh of relief as Myrtle carefully lifted Pasha and set her down softly on the dock.

They walked back up to Myrtle's house with their empty ice cream bowls. Pasha followed for a few seconds before finding something that needed exploring, or perhaps killing, in the bushes.

They loaded the dishes in the dishwasher and Miles yawned. "So later today? We were going to eat lunch and then watch *Tomorrow's Promise*, weren't we?"

"That is the plan. Then I can fill you in on whatever nefarious things Red has planned for me. I'll see you around eleven."

Myrtle woke up around six that morning and stared at her ceiling for a while. But she was wide awake, as usual, so she supposed she must have pieced together enough sleep somehow.

She climbed out of bed, made herself breakfast, and then took on the daily crossword puzzle in the newspaper.

When her doorbell rang at nine, she raised her eyebrows. This was not the appointed time Red had suggested. But it was indeed Red she saw when she looked out the window.

She opened up the door to her son and said in a cheery voice, "Well, hi there. Come on in and get some coffee."

"Sorry I'm not here when I said I was going to be. Jack isn't a happy camper this morning and I thought heading your way early might be the perfect excuse to run away." Red headed into the kitchen and proceeded to fix a very large, sugary cup of coffee.

"Poor Jack. I bet his little teeth are bothering him again." Myrtle believed her grandson could do no wrong.

"I'm not sure it's teeth, Mama. He just woke up on the wrong side of the bed."

Myrtle suspected that Red might have woken on precisely the same, wrong side of the bed, himself. His red hair, now laced with gray, was rumpled as if he'd run his hands through it. And despite the freshly-pressed police uniform he wore, there was already evidence of a coffee stain.

Red settled down at the kitchen table and Myrtle joined him. She forced a grin at him, which made it look as though she was baring her teeth. "So to what do I owe the pleasure of a visit from you today, Red?"

Red gave his mother an earnest look. She was starting to distrust these looks of his. He'd apparently decided that his usual, brusque, heavy-handed approach wasn't working and pulled another method out of his bag of tricks. He clearly wanted her to think that whatever he was about to suggest was in her own best interests.

"I've been thinking about your finances, Mama," he started out, his eyes crinkling at the corners as he forced a smile at her.

Myrtle snorted. "I'm not sure my money situation can be elevated by referring to it as 'finances.' It's simply not grand enough to qualify."

Red chuckled. "Well, at any rate, there is income and there are expenses. Your state pension from teaching comes in and your social security check comes in."

The fact that he was explaining something that Myrtle knew very well was annoying to her. She glowered at him.

Red continued. "Then you have your expenses—the utilities, food, and whatnot."

Myrtle again bared her teeth at him.

"I was thinking that it would be a lot easier on you if we set everything up on automatic draft. That's the way Elaine and I have our payables set up. Our bills are paid automatically and the bank sends out the payment to the biller without us ever having to worry about it."

Myrtle knit her brows. "I'm assuming this has something to do with the fact the power bill went unpaid last month."

Red held out his hands as if to show he had nothing to hide. "Mama, it could happen to anyone. As I said, Elaine and I have our own payables set up that way so we won't overlook anything. With Jack around, we're always distracted and sleep-deprived. And I won't even get started on how sleep-deprived *you* are."

Myrtle said airily, "As I mentioned before, the power bill wasn't paid because of an error on the utility's behalf."

"Uh-huh." Red didn't sound as if he believed this.

"Or, perhaps, an error by the post office. I have noticed incredible issues with them lately."

Red said, "Regardless, this would solve that problem. Because I wasn't crazy about the fact they were threatening to cut your power off—whether it was their error or not."

"Do you know what the inherent drawback with your scheme is?"

Red looked a bit surprised to have auto-payments referred to as a "scheme." He shook his head.

"The drawback is that I wouldn't have control over when that money leaves my checking account. That idea makes me most unhappy."

Red said, "But you *can* choose. You can choose what day the payment from the biller comes out as long as it's not after the duc date."

"Yes, but then that date is set in stone with the company who's pulling out the money, Red. I can't change the payment date in a very agile way. Money isn't a static thing, at least in my household. It ebbs and flows. An auto-draft doesn't take into account the complexities of my pocketbook."

Red took a large slug of his coffee. When he next spoke, the earnestness was replaced by his usual pushiness. "Mama, I don't understand what's so complex about your checking account. You were just arguing your money situation doesn't even qualify as 'finances.'"

"Here's an example, Red. I got one of my checks at the end of last week. But Emma-Jean Cantrell was taking a collection to help with a backpack drive for the less-fortunate kids in the area.

So I had to make some adjustments because, as a former teacher, I like to donate to those types of causes. I gave Emma-Jean fifty dollars and I ate foods out of my freezer until the end of the week. Which wasn't a terrible idea, because there were frozen foods that really needed to be defrosted and eaten. Then I paid my water bill in person at the end of the week when I got paid."

Red rubbed his face. "You gave Emma-Jean Cantrell your grocery and water bill money?"

"Mostly groceries and partly water. But do you see what I'm saying?"

"I'm seeing," said Red, "that you're robbing Peter to pay Paul."

"What you *should* be seeing," said Myrtle in a censorious voice, "is that I have a handle on it. But I don't need any auto-drafts added to the situation. They will create unadulterated chaos."

Red looked as if he might have more to say on the subject, but he wisely took a sip of coffee instead. "Okay," he said in a calming tone. "Moving on. What have you been doing to keep yourself busy these days?"

Red had experienced various times in the past when his mother was bored. These were not, he'd decided, good times. When Myrtle was at loose ends, bad things tended to happen. She'd even orchestrated insurrections at the retirement home.

"Miles and I have been working on the issue of having little to do," said Myrtle with a sniff. "Unfortunately, the heatwave hasn't been helping since we're limited to indoor activities. The events Miles found were fairly pitiful. But this morning before you came, I found a class that I believe I'll enroll in. It should be quite useful."

"A class? That sounds like a good idea." Red latched eagerly onto the idea of his mother safely tucked away in a classroom, under adult supervision. "Gardening? Computers?"

"I understand how to use computers," said Myrtle darkly. "That's a terrible stereotype perpetuated against seniors and one that's not remotely true."

Once again, Red appeared to have more to say on the subject of technology-illiterate seniors but was wisely able to keep his thoughts to himself.

Myrtle continued, "I decided to sign up for a CPR class that will take place next month. Considering your obvious issues with hypertension, I thought it a prudent course of action."

Red's face turned exactly the shade of scarlet that made Myrtle think of the CPR class in the first place.

"You realize," he said coldly, "that the whole reason I *have* a problem with high blood pressure is because of you."

"Then I should be the one to help save you," said Myrtle primly.

Red opened his mouth to discuss this further when his phone rang. He frowned and answered it. "Chief Clover."

Chapter Two

Red listened, his eyebrows drawing together. "Wait, who is it? Luther Cobb. Remind me of the address? You're sure he's dead? What happened?" He listened again, now looking very alert.

Myrtle was looking very alert, too.

"He didn't just choke? I see. I'll be right there." He hung up and said, "Mama, I've got to go."

"Good to see you, sweetie," said Myrtle. She watched as he left and then picked up the phone and called Miles.

Miles had apparently been able to fall back asleep after their nighttime visit. In fact, he sounded very deeply asleep and rather confused. "Mmm?"

"Yes, it's Myrtle. We need to head over to Luther Cobb's place. There's apparently been a murder."

Miles sounded only slightly less-groggy when he said, "Luther Cobb? He's dead? Or someone else?"

"I think it's Luther who's dead, but I'd like to find out more. Can you drive me?" asked Myrtle impatiently.

"Going to take me a couple of minutes to get ready." There was a crashing sound on Mile's end of the line.

"Are you all right, Miles?"

There was a scuffling sound. Miles said, "Yes. Dropped the phone and knocked the lamp off the bedside table."

"I'll have coffee in a travel mug for you," said Myrtle briskly.

About fifteen minutes later, Miles showed up outside. Myrtle joined him in the car and handed him the mug of coffee. Miles took a sip from it.

Myrtle frowned. "Miles, your bleary eyes are concerning me. How about if *I* drive your car? I'm not sure you're alert enough to qualify as a driver."

Miles made protesting noises but Myrtle was quite firm. He finally nodded and they traded places. Myrtle set out down the road at a sedate ten miles an hour.

Miles took another sip of coffee. "Now what's going on?" he asked after a moment or two. "A man is murdered? I'm not sure I know who this guy is. And I'm wondering how on earth you found out about it."

"Red was over having our pre-planned conversation when he got the call. Luther Cobb is the victim and I can't say it's a huge surprise. He's awful when he drinks and he drinks a lot. He probably made someone upset and they decided to silence him once and for all."

"Did Red say how he died?"

"Red didn't say *anything* to me, as usual. He just wanted to discuss automatic drafts for my payables. I was able to pick up a little information by listening in on his one-sided telephone conversation. From what I understand, the death must have been related to something Luther ate. Red asked if he hadn't just choked and the answer seemed to be no."

Miles shifted uncomfortably in the passenger seat. "I don't think Red will be pleased to see us."

"Red was so irritating this morning that I'm happy to provide him with a few unhappy minutes. I'm planning to call Dusty as soon as I get back home. A gnome invasion is imminent."

Miles gave a smile. Whenever Myrtle was unhappy with her son, which was a regular occurrence, she had her yardman pull out her extensive gnome collection into her front yard. Since Red lived directly across the street, it gave an excellent visual representation of her displeasure with him.

At the speed Myrtle was driving, it took a little while to reach Luther Cobb's house. When they arrived, there were already a few emergency vehicles there. Myrtle carefully parked some distance from the property and they peered out at the proceedings.

Myrtle said, "I think we can be useful here, Miles. Which is more than I can say for going to bingo, considering that was another possible activity you listed for today."

"At least it's early enough in the day that it's not broiling outside yet," said Miles with a sigh. He pointed the air conditioning vent directly at himself. But then Myrtle turned off the motor and Miles sighed again. "We're not getting out of the car, are we?"

"Of course we are. We can't be remotely useful if we're sitting down in a vehicle while an awful tragedy transpires yards away."

Miles stared at the emergency vehicles. "I have a feeling that the awful tragedy has already run its course, no matter what we might be doing."

Myrtle opened the door and glanced around. "There's Jasper Hodges."

Miles quirked an eyebrow and followed her gaze. "How do you know everyone in town? I mean, I know it's not a very big town, but *I* certainly don't know everyone here."

Myrtle said absently, "I've lived here my whole life, for one. For another, Jasper was a student of mine. He's Red's age. He looks entirely too interested in the proceedings going on here. Let's go speak with him."

Miles reluctantly followed Myrtle, who was walking with determination toward an athletic-looking man in his late forties with blond hair. The man had been pacing a bit but stopped when he saw Myrtle and Miles headed his way.

"Mrs. Clover," said Jasper, giving her a tight smile. "How are you?"

"Curious," said Myrtle. "Do you know what's going on here at Luther's house?"

Jasper nodded and swallowed. "Luther is dead. And it doesn't look real natural. I mean, it doesn't look *really* natural."

Myrtle was used to people verbally editing themselves when speaking with their former English teacher. She glanced at Miles and said, "Do you know Miles Bradford?"

Jasper reached out a hand and Miles cautiously shook it. He was sure to use his ever-present hand sanitizer at the next discreet opportunity.

"Were you here when Luther was discovered?" asked Myrtle.

Jasper nodded again and swallowed. "Yes. As a matter of fact, I'd just rung the doorbell. I was running over to talk with Luther about something. His wife, Dinah, answered the door and we were together when we found him in the kitchen."

Myrtle pursed her lips. "That must have been very upsetting for Dinah."

Jasper swallowed again. "It was. I think the ambulance guys are giving her a quick check-up just to make sure she's all right."

Miles stared uncomfortably at the emergency vehicles again as if wishing he were anywhere but there.

Myrtle said, "Could you tell what happened by looking at Luther?"

Jasper said slowly, "Well, at first I thought he'd had some kind of medical emergency while he was eating. You know, like a heart attack or a really bad stroke or something. Luther was a big guy with some unhealthy habits and I thought his death might have been due to something natural."

"But now you think it wasn't?"

"That's what I'm wondering. Because it seemed like it had more to do with the food he was eating. Then I was thinking maybe he'd choked or something. But it wasn't really the kind of food that was hard to swallow. When I think about choking hazard foods, I'm mostly thinking about peanut butter with chewy bread or popcorn or maybe hot dogs. But Luther was eating pie."

Myrtle thought about this. "That's interesting. I wouldn't necessarily have thought that was the kind of food that would be hard to eat."

"Right. And the way he looked—I don't want to upset you, Mrs. Clover, but it didn't look like someone who'd just had a tough time swallowing. It looked like the *food* might have killed him."

Miles frowned. "You think he was poisoned?"

Jasper looked at him in surprise, as if having forgotten Miles was there. "That's right. And when the police spoke to me, they acted like they suspected Luther might have been poisoned, too. There was a note next to the pie—somebody else had brought it in. It wasn't like Dinah had baked the pie."

"A note? So the pie might have been dropped off by someone?" asked Miles.

"Exactly."

Myrtle said, "What did the note say?"

Jasper said, "That's the thing. It said 'thinking of you.' And it wasn't signed."

Myrtle's eyes opened wide. "So someone left a pie for Luther, dropped it off at the house, and didn't even put their name on it?"

"Right." Jasper shook his head and shrugged. "Crazy, isn't it? Dinah hadn't been home when it was dropped off."

"Did she have any other information about the pie or why someone would have dropped it by?" asked Myrtle.

"She was really, really upset, Mrs. Clover. But she calmed down a little after I called Red and before he came over. Dinah said Luther had been ailing lately because he had a car accident and had surgery after it. People had been bringing food by to help Dinah out because she'd been spending time taking care of him."

Myrtle said slowly, "But it seems that someone might have accidentally killed Dinah also if they dropped by a poisoned pie."

Jasper shook his head again. "Maybe not. Because right before the cops came over, she said that good friends generally knew that she didn't eat sweets. Just never had the taste for them. I guess that's one reason why she's thin as a rail. So anybody who wanted to get rid of Luther would have known Dinah wouldn't be accidentally eating the pie."

Myrtle tilted her head to one side and considered Jasper with a look that made him revert back to days in the classroom. "Might I ask, Jasper, what *you* were doing here? Were you friends with Luther?"

He reddened a bit. "No, I wouldn't exactly call us friends."

"Is that why you carried a gun over here?" asked Myrtle smoothly.

Miles drew back a little. Just the thought of shaking hands with someone toting a gun made him dig through his pockets for his hand sanitizer, which he applied liberally.

Jasper gave Myrtle a grudgingly admiring look. "You are very observant, Mrs. Clover."

"I'm sure Red was, too," said Myrtle dryly.

"Yes ma'am, he wanted to check on my conceal carry permit right away. But it was all good—I'm certified and it's current."

Myrtle cared very little about the status of Jasper's paperwork. She was a lot more interested to hear why Jasper had gone over to Luther's house with a gun. She raised her eyebrows and just waited.

Jasper looked down at his shoes. "That's the problem, isn't it? It just doesn't look real good. That's what the police think, too, I'm sure. I just came over because I'd heard Luther treating Dinah pretty bad yesterday when they were out at the store. The way he was talking to her was awful. I thought somebody should stand up for her, that's all. She doesn't have any family in town or anything. So I thought about it for a while and then decided to come over and confront him."

"With a gun."

Jasper swallowed. "He was a big guy, Mrs. Clover. I didn't fancy my chances with him."

"But you just finished saying that Dinah was taking care of him because he was recovering from surgery following a car accident."

Jasper looked at her admiringly. "You're still sharp as a tack, Mrs. Clover."

Myrtle just waited, eyes narrowed.

Jasper took a deep breath. "Yeah, he was injured. But that's how much of a control freak he was. He was at the store, on crutches, with Dinah to make sure she got exactly what he wanted her to pick up there. And this morning, I thought I'd wear my gun just to intimidate him, you know?"

"But he was dead when you arrived," said Myrtle.

"That's right. Then I called the cops and tried to calm down Dinah and here we are." He gave a small shrug and looked morosely at the emergency vehicles. He looked at his watch and shook his head. "Well, I need to get on to work. I was hanging around because I thought I should make sure Dinah was okay, but it looks like the cops are still talking to her."

Myrtle said smoothly, "Don't worry. We'll check in on her, Jasper."

He hesitated for a moment before giving a quick nod. "Got it. I'll head out, then."

After he left, Myrtle and Miles watched the scene from a distance for a few minutes. Miles said, "Did you get the impression that he wasn't telling the whole story?"

"I most certainly did. I almost expected his nose to start growing with all the lies."

Miles lifted an eyebrow. "Did you think he was lying, then? I thought maybe they were just omissions."

"I think he was lying about why he was over at Luther's house, yes. I don't think of Jasper as somebody who really looks out for others' interests if they don't impact him. And yet he was over here to protect Dinah out of the goodness of his heart?" Myrtle shook her head.

"Why do you think he came over here, then?"

Myrtle said, "If I had to guess, it has something to do with that teenager of his. Archie, I think his name is. Jasper thinks the sun and moon rise in that child. Whenever I see Jasper out around town, he always has Archie with him. And I think this conversation we had with him might be the only one where he wasn't bragging about Archie."

Miles said, "Archie is apparently brag-worthy?"

"According to Jasper, he definitely is. From what I remember, Archie is something of an athletic superstar. Baseball, maybe? Or maybe it was soccer. Anyway, he's in the midst of college recruitment and Jasper is heavily involved in all that." Myrtle glanced down the street and said, "Look, Dinah is finished speaking with Red."

Miles looked leery. "Myrtle, she's just endured a terrible tragedy."

"I'm thinking she was well-rid of Luther if he was treating her so shabbily. Besides, we just promised Jasper that we'd follow-up to make sure Dinah was doing all right."

Myrtle started walking down the sidewalk toward Dinah and Miles reluctantly followed.

They didn't get too close to the scene, but were close enough so that Red glowered at his mother and made a sweeping motion with his hands to indicate that she needed to stay back. Fortunately, it was at that moment that Dinah spotted them and started moving their way.

Chapter Three

"Miss Myrtle," Dinah called out. She was a tall, thin woman with graying brown hair that she had pulled back into a ponytail. Her eyes were red and she had every appearance of being completely exhausted from what had just transpired.

Myrtle said, "My dear. I was with Red when he got the phone call and I immediately came over. Do you need to sit down? We have Miles's car here."

Dinah gave her a grateful look. "Do you mind? I've been feeling like my legs won't be able to hold me up much longer. But I can't go into the house, because ... well ..." She gestured over to the house and the crowd of police there.

Miles quickly opened the car door and Dinah sat down with relief. "Thank you so much." She hesitated. "I guess you heard what happened."

Myrtle nodded. "After a fashion. Jasper filled us in a little bit."

Dinah had an expression on her face as if she wasn't sure Jasper's version was something she wanted spread around. "Did he? What did Jasper say?"

Myrtle said, "He was saying that he'd come by to talk to Luther about something and that the two of you discovered Luther in the kitchen. That he'd been eating a pie that had an anonymous note."

Dinah nodded wearily. "Awful. Everyone's been so kind, bringing food by. This pie was sitting outside our house this morning with a note and I just figured it was another sweet gesture from one of our friends. But instead, somebody must have put poison in it." She frowned. "Actually, I took a picture of the pie this morning. It looked so sweet just sitting on the step."

"Could you possibly send that photo to me?" asked Myrtle.

Dinah looked slightly confused but, like most people, did what Myrtle asked. Myrtle recited her phone number to her and Dinah texted the picture over.

"Jasper seemed to think that Luther hadn't had a natural death," Myrtle said.

Dinah shook her head helplessly. "Apparently not. It didn't look like he'd choked. And from what the police said, it didn't look like he'd had a heart attack or anything. It's so hard to understand."

Miles said carefully, "It was good that you had Jasper here with you. That must have been very upsetting."

"Shocking," said Dinah in a sober tone. "It's good that Jasper happened to be here."

Myrtle asked, "And why was he here, dear?"

Dinah sighed. "Well, Luther has been a little bit of a trial lately. The car accident and surgery really frustrated him. You know how he always had that take-charge attitude. He liked to be in control of things."

Myrtle had the feeling that Luther had very much liked being in charge of *people*, as well.

"Anyway, the point is that Luther has been very frustrated lately because of his lack of mobility."

Miles, remembering Jasper's tale of encountering Luther in the grocery store, asked, "He hasn't been mobile at all?"

"He's gotten around some, but not to the extent that he normally has. Like I said, it made him frustrated and that frustration led him to act out a bit." Thinking of this made Dinah look even more exhausted than she already did.

"And he acted out with Jasper?" asked Myrtle.

Dinah sighed. "I'm afraid so. You know how Jasper is crazy about that boy."

"I know that he thinks Archie has quite a future and might get an athletic scholarship to college."

Dinah nodded. "Well, of course, what it boils down to is that Archie is still just a teenager. Archie's life is probably super-disciplined. He has to get up in the morning very early and exercise before school, according to Jasper. Then he goes to school, goes to hours of practice, and then goes home to *more* hours of homework. So it probably wasn't any real surprise when Luther saw him doing something he wasn't supposed to do. Archie probably was trying to rebel, in a small way."

Myrtle raised her eyebrows. "Archie was doing something that might jeopardize his future?"

Dinah shrugged. "I guess, Miss Myrtle. Jasper sure seemed to think so. I was driving Luther to a doctor appointment and Luther said, 'Isn't that Archie Hodges?' Luther always followed the high school sports, you see. And I looked over and nodded.

Luther was like, 'Wonder why he's not in school? It's a school day.' And that's when we saw Archie and a friend of his spray-painting one of the beautiful old buildings downtown."

Myrtle raised her eyebrows. "Downtown? In the hub of the town? That seems rather reckless and bold of him."

Dinah sighed again. "Maybe it was a sort of cry for help? That poor kid doesn't sound like he has much of a life at all."

Miles said slowly, "What happened after you and Luther saw Archie vandalizing the building?"

"Well, I felt sorry for Archie. I thought the most appropriate thing to do would be to call Jasper and let him know what we'd seen. But Luther wouldn't hear of it." She pressed her lips together in a tight line, remembering.

"He wanted to tell the police," guessed Myrtle.

"Even worse," said Dinah. "He wanted to tell Jasper that he was *planning* on talking to the police."

Myrtle and Miles considered this for a moment.

"So the point of that exercise," said Myrtle, "was to feel a sense of control over Archie's future, I'm guessing."

"I'm afraid so. It wasn't that he wanted to blackmail Jasper. It was more that he wanted to enjoy the sense of being able to close the door on Archie's promising future. When Luther is bored, like he was during the last couple of weeks, he can be very . . . mischievous."

Myrtle could think of other words that would better describe Luther's actions. From Miles's expression, he could, too.

Myrtle said, "And then Jasper came over here with a gun to talk to Luther."

Dinah looked rather alarmed. "Did he have a gun?"

"He was wearing it when I talked to him."

Dinah knit her brows together. "But why would he have done that if he'd already poisoned Luther?"

Miles nodded. "Why would he even come by the house at all?"

Dinah shrugged. "I don't know. It doesn't really make sense. It makes it look as if Jasper couldn't have had anything to do with it."

"Maybe that was by design," said Myrtle. She pressed her lips together. "Aside from Jasper, did anyone else have an issue with Luther?"

Dinah's eyes were sad. "I'm afraid plenty of people did. Like I said, when Luther wasn't feeling well, he really wasn't himself. But the person who most comes to mind is Vivian."

"Is that Vivian Lawson?" asked Myrtle.

"That's right. She was Luther's assistant. For *years*." Dinah paused and her brow puckered. "Oh, heavens. I suppose I should let her know."

Myrtle said, "I'm sure she'll have a lot of work to do, wrapping up Luther's business concerns."

Dinah shook her head slowly. "No, because Luther fired her recently. I'm sure that made her very unhappy, as it should have. I have the feeling that Luther was being very unreasonable. Vivian had been working for him for ages, though, and is someone I should probably notify. I felt so sorry for her when he fired her. I can imagine that Vivian was very upset with him."

"Does she bake pies?" asked Myrtle archly.

"As a matter of fact, I think she's supposed to be an excellent cook in every way. We've talked about it before."

Myrtle took out her phone and opened the text message that Dinah had sent her a couple of minutes ago. She frowned at the image and Miles peered over her shoulder at it.

Myrtle said, "That is definitely a store-bought pie. There's no question, that is not homemade."

Dinah's brow crinkled in confusion. "Are you sure?"

"Positive," said Myrtle crisply.

Miles added, "Myrtle sometimes buys store bought pies to bring to book club." He managed to keep a completely straight face.

"Baking can be challenging," said Myrtle. "It's sort of like a science experiment. Sometimes I don't have time to be a scientist."

Dinah was still trying to figure out the implications of the pie being store-bought. "The store is selling poisoned pies?"

"I think the more-likely explanation is that someone purchased the pie at the store and then proceeded to insert something poisonous," said Myrtle.

Dinah looked somber. "Who could have hated him that much?"

"Not Vivian?" asked Myrtle.

"I can believe she was angry with Luther and probably rightfully so. But I just can't imagine her putting poison in a pie for him to eat."

Myrtle asked, "Did Vivian know that you're not fond of sweets?"

Dinah looked rueful. "Anyone who knows me well does. It's such an unusual thing, not having a sweet tooth. Vivian certainly did, yes." She glanced over at the house and said, "I think they're motioning me over to ask me a question."

Myrtle said, "We'll check on you later, Dinah. We're very sorry about Luther."

Dinah walked quickly out of earshot and Miles said, "*Are* we very sorry about Luther?"

"Not really," said Myrtle coolly. "I always thought he was something of a bully. I can't abide bullies. But I would like to find out what happened to him. I'm sure Dinah is falling under suspicion and she's really a lovely person. We must clear this up so everyone in Bradley isn't looking at Dinah as if she killed her husband."

Dinah was speaking with one of the state police officers who seemed to be taking a lot of notes. Red, who was nearby, glowered again at Myrtle when he saw her. She gave him a cheery wave.

Miles said dryly, "If you're so concerned about Red's health, we should probably get out of here. He looks distinctly unamused by our presence."

"Not quite yet. I'd like to ask him some questions about the pie." Myrtle leaned against Miles's car, with every appearance of being there for the long-haul. She glanced at Miles. "At least you're looking a little perkier. Although you should probably have a little more of your coffee."

Miles gave the travel mug a leery look. "That was very strong coffee, Myrtle."

"It was meant to be curative. The type of coffee that serves a function. You definitely needed to wake up."

Miles said dryly, "Well, I'm awake now. In fact, I think my heart is racing."

Myrtle squinted across the road and said, "Red is coming over. Excellent."

Miles wasn't at all sure it was excellent. Red looked decidedly unhappy at their being on the scene. "Maybe we should hop back into the car and tell him we were just driving by on our way to breakfast."

"Don't be silly, Miles. I need to ask him some questions."

Miles lifted an eyebrow. "Do you really think he'll give us any information? If you're too nosy, Red might leap on the excuse to cart you off to Greener Pastures."

Myrtle said darkly, "I'd like to see him try."

Red hurried up and said, "Mama, this is the very last place in Bradley you should be right now."

She gave him a sweet smile. "Now, you know I couldn't resist coming over. You got the call when you were at my house. I'm not sure how you thought I was simply going to ignore that."

"This is a crime scene." Red glowered at her.

"Is it? Well, it's good to get that part verified by an official. Although it certainly sounded that way from what Jasper and Dinah were saying. A pie, wasn't it? A rather clever idea. It sounds as if it was doctored up by whomever wanted to kill Luther. I understand the pie was poisoned."

Red glared at her. "Nothing has been tested yet."

"Naturally. But I'm imagining you and your team were making inferences from what you saw in the house. You've already labeled this a crime scene, so it's clear that Luther didn't die from natural causes. Considering the fact that he was eating a pie at the time of his unexpected demise, it does seem to boil down to poison."

Red rubbed his hands over his eyes, looking very much as if he wanted to get back to bed and start the day over again. "I can't discuss this with you." He turned to Miles and said, "How about if you take my mother for a nice breakfast?" He fumbled in his pockets until he found his battered wallet. "Here's some cash for her meal. Since her financial situation is . . . complex." He gave Myrtle a dour look.

She gave a triumphant smile. "At least you're getting the full picture now."

Miles pocketed the money and said, "Thanks, Red."

"No, thank *you*. For putting up with my mother's craziness and taking her out for breakfast." One of the state police officers called out to Red and he held up a finger to indicate he'd be there in a minute. "Before y'all go, tell me what you heard from Jasper and Dinah."

Myrtle gave him an arch look. "Haven't you spoken to them already?"

"Yes. But I have the feeling that someone who isn't wearing a police uniform might have gotten completely different responses."

Miles shifted uncomfortably. He was certain that Myrtle wouldn't want to disclose anything from their conversations with Jasper or Dinah. She preferred to solve the cases herself and viewed Red as competition. Or, perhaps, an obstacle to her goals.

Indeed, Myrtle was giving her son a crafty look. "Red, I don't know what you're talking about. Jasper came over to make a little small talk while he was waiting for the police to dismiss him."

Red snorted. "Small talk. At a crime scene."

"Precisely. Sometimes you need to have a little time to extrapolate and decompress after having discovered a body in the middle of what had been a normal morning."

Red nodded. "That's exactly what I'm looking for—what was extrapolated from your conversation with Jasper. Dinah, too."

Myrtle pretended to mull this over. "I'd said that Jasper was feeling . . . sad. And reflective over the fact that our grasp on life is tenuous at best." She turned to Miles. "It seemed to me that Jasper was heading back out with a new lease on life. Didn't it seem that way to you?"

Miles gave a quick, unhappy nod of agreement.

Red was back to rubbing his face again. "So you were talking about philosophical issues surrounding death. I didn't realize Jasper had that kind of depth. He's always been sort of a jock."

"You're sounding very sarcastic, Red. The man was shaken up and naturally was trying to sort out his feelings about the entire episode."

"And Luther's wife, Dinah? Did you also discuss life and death with her?"

Myrtle said, "Only in the broadest sense. She has quite a bit of adjusting to do, you know. Dinah has labeled herself as 'Luther's wife' for decades and now she's having to rethink exactly who she *is* now. It's quite a change, isn't it?"

Red gave her a suspicious look and Myrtle smiled pleasantly in return. He said, "The only reason I'm not pursuing this further right now is because someone needs to speak with me. But I have the sinking suspicion that you likely asked Jasper and Dinah a bunch of questions. I don't want you to be pretending to be Miss Marple again."

He gave Miles a weary look and then stomped off toward the other police officers.

Chapter Four

Myrtle snorted. "Who has to *pretend* to be Miss Marple? I've already gotten a lot more information than Red could ever dream of."

Miles gestured toward the car. "Can we go? I don't think we're going to get any more answers by hanging out here now."

But Myrtle had spotted something. "You can wait for me in the car, if you want. I see Lieutenant Perkins just made it here."

Miles sighed. "Don't you think Perkins will be busy assessing the scene or whatever it is that ranking state police officers do?"

"I believe the scene has already been assessed," said Myrtle, walking with determination toward the tall, wiry man with the military haircut.

Red, fortunately, had not seen his mother progress toward Perkins and he walked up to speak with him. Myrtle could tell Red was explaining what had happened as he gestured toward different things. Myrtle figured there was a good chance for her to listen in, undetected.

They were faced away from her, looking toward Luther's house as she approached. She could hear Red saying, "The thing is, there's a botanist nearby. Ezra Blake. He probably has all kinds of poisonous plants over there at the ready."

Perkins said in his measured voice, "Was he someone with a motive?"

Myrtle hung back and waited for a moment.

Red shrugged. "Not that I know of, but it's definitely a line of inquiry I think we should explore." He suddenly stiffened and whirled around, eyes narrowing as he caught sight of Myrtle.

Myrtle gave him a cheerful smile. "Hi there!"

"Mama! I thought you were on your way to breakfast."

Myrtle said, "Now you know I couldn't leave without saying hello to my old friend."

Lt. Perkins, always exceedingly courteous, even at an active crime scene, said, "Mrs. Clover, it's such a pleasure to see you. Despite the circumstances."

Red rubbed his forehead as if it was hurting him.

Myrtle gave Perkins an enthusiastic hug, knocking him slightly off-balance. "Perkins! I was just thinking about you the other day. Miles is going to be part of a chess tournament locally and I thought to myself that *you* were probably an excellent chess player. You should join in or at least watch the tournament. You're such a smart man; I figure you're probably great at the game."

Red said darkly, "Mama, Lt. Perkins doesn't have time to play chess."

"I'm afraid that's probably correct, Mrs. Clover," said Perkins regretfully. "Although it sounds like a lot of fun."

"So you *do* play," said Myrtle triumphantly.

"Guilty as charged."

"I thought so. Well, maybe we can wrap up this case quickly so you can participate." Myrtle gave him a smile.

Red intoned, "There's no *we* when it comes to the case. The police are handling this investigation."

Red gave Perkins a look and Perkins quickly added, "That's true. Mrs. Clover, I'm sure we'll be able to wrap up this case soon—perhaps even in time for me to watch the tournament."

"Excellent!"

Red said, "And now it's time for you to leave, Mama. You and Miles are heading to the diner, remember?"

"Right. Well, toodle-oo, Perkins!" Myrtle beamed at the lieutenant. Then she looked at Red crossly and said, "See you later, Red."

She walked back to the car where Miles, apparently wired on caffeine, was now sitting behind the wheel and looking a bit jittery. As soon as Myrtle sat in the passenger seat, Miles quickly drove off, as if trying to prevent Myrtle from accosting anyone else.

"So, the diner, right?" asked Miles.

"Apparently," said Myrtle distractedly.

"How was Perkins?"

Myrtle said, "He was just fine. We were able to chat a little bit. He might be able play chess with you."

"What?"

"Well, not right this second, obviously, considering a murder has just occurred. But he sounded very interested in your chess tournament, most likely as a spectator. He plays the game."

Miles looked as if he didn't fancy his chances playing against Perkins. "Sounds great," he said without enthusiasm.

They reached the diner quickly and were able to get a booth without any wait. The diner had been in downtown Bradley since Myrtle was a girl. There were laminate floors, menus, and tables. A sign on the wall stated: *The language you use in church is good enough to use in here.* Myrtle had the menu memorized.

The waitress came over and said, "Hi loves. What can I get you to eat?"

Miles was still studying the menu as if cramming for a final exam. Myrtle said, "Miles, how much money did Red give you for the two of us?"

Miles said, "Enough for you to order whatever you like."

Myrtle beamed. "All right then. I'll have the lumberjack breakfast."

The waitress jotted this down on her notepad. "With grits or hashbrowns, love?"

"Grits *and* hashbrowns, please. The surcharge is no problem."

"Toast or a biscuit?"

"Both," said Myrtle as her stomach growled at the delectable thought.

The waitress raised a well-drawn eyebrow. "And you'd like bacon *and* sausage?"

"Why not? At my age, one shouldn't have to eat a bunch of health food."

"No danger of that," muttered Miles.

The waitress, sensing a nice tip, was very cheerful. "And how do you want your eggs, darlin'?"

"Scrambled, please."

The waitress turned to Miles. "And you, sweetie?"

Miles cleared his throat. "May I have a glass of cranberry juice? And perhaps a bowl of oatmeal?"

Myrtle gave him a disgusted look.

"Of course you can, love." The waitress noted his order on her pad, gave them a smile and headed off to place the order.

"Miles, you're becoming positively monk-like."

He said, "I don't believe monks eat oatmeal and drink cranberry juice, do they?"

"Gruel, oatmeal . . . it's all the same. We're not young people, Miles. We should live however we please."

Miles said, "Well, I'm thinking I'd like to extend my stay on Earth by just a little bit." He noticed the individual packages of jams and jellies were in a heap on the side of the table and carefully started stacking them by flavor in neat rows. "How did your conversation with Perkins go? Aside from chess."

"What was more interesting was the conversation that Red and Perkins were having before I interrupted them," said Myrtle with satisfaction.

"You were able to do a little eavesdropping then?" Miles didn't sound at all surprised at this information.

"That's right. Red was talking about our friend, Ezra Blake. He's apparently on Red's list of suspects, which I do think is rather shortsighted of Red."

Miles said slowly, "Well, he is a botanist. I suppose it makes sense that he might be a suspect. After all, not only would he likely have access to poisonous plants, he'd know exactly what type of reaction the poison would cause."

"He would. But Red is leaping to conclusions, which is something he's fond of doing." Myrtle's mouth tightened in dissatisfaction. "Perhaps it's time to pay Ezra a visit."

This idea appeared to worry Miles. "On what grounds?"

"On what *grounds*? You sound like we're preparing to sue him, Miles. We're just going to pay him a friendly little visit."

Miles said, "A friendly little visit that's completely out of the blue."

"We're senior citizens. We don't need reasons to do anything. We simply do them. Age has its privileges."

Their food arrived with Myrtle's on multiple plates. The waitress plopped Miles's juice and oatmeal down in front of him and he stared at them with a crestfallen expression.

Myrtle quirked a brow at him. "You can have some of my lumberjack breakfast, if you want. You know you want to."

Indeed, Miles was gazing quite covetously at the generous spread of food in front of Myrtle. "Maybe just the biscuit."

"Sure," said Myrtle, rolling her eyes. "Live a little."

Miles plucked a fluffy biscuit off a plate and then took one of the jelly packets he'd carefully stacked and doctored it up. He said, "What did you think about what Dinah said?"

Myrtle swallowed a bite of bacon and took a sip of coffee. "I thought it was very interesting that her account of what Jasper had been doing there was so different from his own story."

"I didn't totally understand the connection between Luther and Jasper. They seem like people whose paths wouldn't cross much in real life." Miles took a large bite of his biscuit and looked very happy. "I was surprised that Luther would even know who Archie is."

"Remember, Luther followed local sports. He was very interested in the different teams. With Archie being something of a standout, I'm sure he followed his progress in the paper." Myrtle ate her scrambled eggs for a few quiet minutes while she thought things through. "Jasper is so invested in Archie that I know he'd be desperate not to let anything jeopardize his future."

"Wouldn't it jeopardize his future to have his father arrested for murder, though? Coming over with a gun is very heavy-handed, isn't it?" Having eaten his biscuit, Miles looked glumly at the bowl of lumpy oatmeal.

"I'm not sure Jasper intended on *using* the gun. I think it's more likely that he wanted a way to intimidate Luther and he decided that would be the way to do it. He must have planned on going in there, confronting Luther, making a plea for Luther to just keep the information about Archie's vandalism to himself, and getting out of there. Instead, he discovered Luther's body."

Miles frowned. "That's something else that confuses me. Shouldn't Dinah have discovered his body before then?"

"I have the feeling Dinah often gave Luther wide berth. He was a difficult man and she was already spending a good deal of time with him following his car accident. Perhaps she was just relieved that he was giving her what seemed like a quiet morning."

Miles shoved his oatmeal around the bowl with his spoon.

"For heaven's sake, Miles, just order something else. They'll have the food to you in fewer than ten minutes and we're in no hurry."

Miles looked unhappily at his food. "Maybe it would be better with some cinnamon sprinkles added to it."

"Maybe it would be better if it magically turned into a plate of eggs, bacon, and biscuits."

The waitress came up to check on them again and looked at Miles's oatmeal with sympathy. "Hey there, baby. Want something different?"

Miles hesitated. "I hate to cause any bother."

Myrtle swiftly said, "I think Miles is just envious of all the delicious food that *I* have and he needs some of his own."

"Another lumberjack breakfast?" asked the waitress, looking very pleased at the tab and her tip going up.

"That's too much food," said Miles.

"I'm planning on packing some of mine in to-go boxes for lunch. You just have to make sure you eat your eggs because they won't reheat well."

Miles gave a small smile to the waitress. "Yes, please. I'll have a lumberjack breakfast."

After the waitress left, Myrtle said, "There was also the matter of Vivian Lawson. Dinah brought up the fact that she might have some grievances against Luther."

Miles pushed his bowl of oatmeal to the side with relief. "Ah. His long-suffering assistant."

"Right. The assistant who bakes things. However, that pie, as I mentioned earlier, was decidedly store-bought. So being a baker is certainly not a prerequisite for this particular crime."

Miles sipped on his cranberry juice thoughtfully. "So the theory is that Vivian Lawson was unhappy about unfairly being fired. She decided to get revenge on Luther by killing him with a poisoned pie."

"It all sounds rather dramatic, doesn't it? Still, I'm sure she wasn't happy about losing a source of income. Her *only* source of income probably. He must have left her in a terrible state. And that could have really stung, especially if she thought it was without merit." Myrtle finished her sausage and then sat back in the booth, feeling full. "What we really need to do is find out more about the poison in that pie. Which is why a friendly visit to Ezra will work out so well."

Miles said, "So we're going with the assumption that it wasn't something like rat poison. That it was a natural, botanical poison."

"Precisely. That assumption is just based on what I over-heard Red saying to Perkins. I do have that photo of the pie and I don't recognize the berries in the picture whatsoever."

Miles knit his brows together. "That's interesting. Could I see the picture?"

Myrtle handed over her phone and Miles peered at the pho-to. "No, I don't, either. They're not blueberries, raspberries, or strawberries, that's for sure."

"Nor blackberries or huckleberries." Myrtle took her phone back and studied the picture again. "The whole design of the pie and the latticework of the pastry on top would have made it very easy to insert the poisoned berries."

"True. It's not like a closed-crust pie." He considered the berry problem again. "Elderberries? Are those elderberries?"

"They're not. No, they're completely unidentifiable. By us, anyway. I'm sure Luther just thought he'd have a lovely piece of pie for breakfast. It looks completely innocuous."

Miles said, "Maybe. But the accompanying note gives me the shivers."

"The *thinking of you* message? Yes, that's pretty creepy."

Miles's food arrived on several plates. He immediately said, "Could I have a to-go box, too?"

"One step ahead of you, love," said the waitress as she put a couple of takeout containers on the table. "Thought you both might need these. And here's the check, whenever you're ready."

The waitress hurried off to another table and Myrtle said, "Now *that* looks like a real breakfast. None of that lumpy oatmeal stuff."

Miles seemed to agree with her, judging from how quickly he made a good deal of his order disappear. When he reached a stopping place, he walked up to the register to pay for their food while Myrtle packed their leftovers into boxes.

Chapter Five

They walked out to Miles's car and he said, "Home?" in a hopeful voice.

"Certainly. We have to put our containers into the fridge. Plus, I want to speak with Dusty before we visit with Ezra."

Miles started up the car. "Does your grass need mowing?"

"Not particularly, although that would be a good idea, considering I want the gnomes pulled out. It does make things look tidier to have the grass cut low. But mostly, I want him to pull out all the gnomes. I need to make a statement to Red."

Miles reflected that the statement Myrtle would make would be more to the entire neighborhood. However, he wisely kept this sentiment to himself.

They put their take-out in Myrtle's fridge and settled in her living room. She pulled out her phone and dialed Dusty.

He answered the phone with a howl. "Can't mow, Miz Myrtle!"

"Dusty, I simply can't have both you *and* Puddin being noncompliant. It's tough enough to get Puddin to even come out to the house without you joining in her nonsense. Besides, I mostly just want you to pull the gnomes out for me. Mowing would have just been a bonus."

"Can't pull out them gnomes neither, Miz Myrtle."

Myrtle closed her eyes briefly. "What's happened now?"

"My back is thrown."

"Dusty, that's Puddin's excuse, not yours. I feel it would be more responsible and creative of you to come up with your own excuses for getting out of work."

Dusty growled, "Well, my back *is* thrown."

"I wasn't aware that was a contagious condition."

"It happened when I was at Miz Darst's house. She had me pulling up a dead bush. It didn't want to pull up."

Myrtle sighed in irritation. "Well, that was most inconsiderate of Darlene Darst to mess up your back just when I needed your help. But just the kind of thing I'd expect from her."

Miles hid a smile. He had the feeling that Myrtle was going to give Darlene a piece of her mind the next time she saw her.

Dusty now sounded a bit penitent. "Tell you what. How about Puddin helps you pull them gnomes out?"

There were wild protestations in the background on the other end of the line. Puddin apparently didn't like that suggestion one bit.

Myrtle said quickly, "I think that's an excellent idea. It sounds like she's at home so this is the perfect time."

There was more squabbling on the other end of the line. Then Puddin apparently wrested the phone out of Dusty's hand.

"My back is thrown, too!" she spat out.

"Highly unlikely," said Myrtle coolly. "Dusty and I just established the condition isn't contagious."

Puddin said in a resentful voice, "Speak English."

"You didn't catch a thrown back from Dusty. And I'm quite sure you weren't pulling dead bushes out of the ground at Darlene Darst's. So you can come right over and help with the gnomes."

"What did he do now?" asked Puddin curiously.

"Red would like to insert himself in my financial affairs."

Puddin tried to sort this out. "So, he wants to take over your money?"

"Something like that. At any rate, it was very inappropriate that he didn't realize I'm sovereign over my own financial arrangements."

Puddin decided to return to the gnomes. "Can't pull out them gnomes by myself, Miz Myrtle."

Myrtle sighed. "No, I expect you can't. But you can help Miles and me pull them out."

Miles, settled on the sofa, gave her a dismayed look.

Puddin grouched, "I guess I'll come on over."

"Thank you. It shouldn't take long." And then Myrtle hung up.

Miles said, "It shouldn't take long? It takes Dusty a full couple of hours to drag those things out of your storage shed and put them strategically around the yard. And you said you wanted a large display."

"Well, I'm going to have to scale things back if Dusty isn't available. It will have to be more of a quieter statement."

Miles said, "And how on earth are you supposed to help with the process? The last thing you need to be doing is trying to balance a cane in one hand and a gnome in the other as you walk across soft ground."

Myrtle glowered at him. "I'm starting to think that I might want to put my gnomes in *your* yard as a statement. And, to answer your question, I happen to have a little red wagon. Puddin can place a gnome in the little wagon and I can pull it over to you. We'll set up sort of an assembly line."

Miles did not look at all pleased at the prospect of an assembly line in Myrtle's yard. Especially one that involved him in any way.

Soon, however, Myrtle heard a loud engine and muffler outside, alerting her to Puddin's arrival. There was a knock at the door and the dour, pasty-faced Puddin scowled at her on her doorstep.

"Good! Now we can get started." Myrtle clapped her hands together.

Miles and Puddin gave her recalcitrant looks.

"It's going to be fun," proclaimed Myrtle. "We can even play music."

This idea was apparently of interest to Puddin. "What kinda music?"

"Whatever kind of music will make you work faster and longer," said Myrtle.

Puddin said craftily, "I got some music on my phone we could listen to."

Miles, an aficionado of both classical and jazz, looked concerned by this idea.

Myrtle, however, gave a breezy, unworried shrug. "Whatever gets the job done."

Which is how they all ended up listening to very hard rock music in Myrtle's yard.

Myrtle, after a few minutes, said, "I may have to disqualify what you have us listening to as an option, Puddin. I don't believe it's music."

"It is! It's metal." Puddin's face was complacent and she bobbed her head up and down in time to the beat.

"Metal is a material," said Myrtle. "Or possibly an element."

"And music," persisted Puddin.

"That is a matter of opinion. At any rate, I need you to turn it down so I can explain how this process is going to work."

Puddin drawled, "Good. 'Cause I can't see how you're planning on lugging gnomes around the yard."

Myrtle ignored her and pulled a shiny red wagon out of the storage shed. "Step one is Puddin loading a gnome into the wagon. Step two is me—I will pull the wagon to Miles's location in the front yard."

Miles looked dejectedly at the wagon.

"Miles will unload the gnome and place it. Then I will return to Puddin and the process will be completed," said Myrtle. "Got it?"

Puddin, who looked distracted by Pasha-the-feral-cat's sudden appearance, gave a vague nod as she followed the cat's movements suspiciously. Pasha plopped down in a sunbeam near Puddin and started grooming herself.

Miles started walking toward Myrtle's front yard. Puddin was still watching Pasha. Pasha stopped giving herself a bath and returned Puddin's stare with green eyes glinting in the sun.

Myrtle frowned. "Puddin, you have to start the process."

"Oh." She edged away from Pasha and looked uncomprehendingly at the storage shed, the gnomes, and the wagon. "Do what, now?"

"Pay attention! Find a gnome that will fit in the wagon. Put it in the wagon."

"Okay, okay," muttered Puddin. She grabbed a random gnome and stuck it in the wagon.

By the time Myrtle returned to Puddin and the shed, Puddin was taking a selfie of herself sticking her tongue out with one of Myrtle's gnomes.

Myrtle gritted her teeth. "Another gnome, Puddin."

Pasha watched with interest as Puddin loaded a gnome wearing sunglasses and a leather jacket into the wagon.

"Do me a favor while I take this to Miles. Find the most obnoxious gnomes and line them up so you're ready when I come back," said Myrtle. "The whole point is to enrage Red."

This seemed to interest Puddin and she was studying the various options in the shed as Myrtle rolled the wagon away.

After about thirty minutes, Myrtle surveyed her front yard. "What do you think of the gnome coverage, Miles?"

Miles peered around him. "Considering the amount of time we've put in, I believe the number of gnomes is probably commiserate with your level of irritation with Red."

"I don't think that's true because I'm *quite* annoyed at Red. But I do think what we've done has made a statement. I suppose I'll go ahead and tell Puddin we can stop for the day."

Puddin didn't have to be told twice. She carefully edged away from Pasha and walked to the front yard, keeping an eye on her back the whole while.

They joined Miles in the front yard. Puddin narrowed her eyes and gave the yard a critically appraising look. "Ain't as good as what Dusty does." She sniffed.

"Well, as soon as Dusty catches that thrown back of his, maybe he can do some rearranging. This was the best the three of us could manage," said Myrtle crisply.

"Oh, I think it looks fabulous!" a voice called out behind them.

They turned to see Elaine and Jack coming across the street. Jack made a crowing sound and hugged his favorite gnome—one carrying a fishing pole and a picnic basket.

Puddin preened at the compliment from Elaine. "We done the best we could. Dusty is hurt."

"I'm sorry to hear that. But it really does look great. And I'm glad to catch y'all because I wanted to ask something about a new hobby of mine."

Puddin looked alarmed. "Well, gotta go check on Dusty. I'll let y'all talk about the hobby. Hope you have a good one." And she made a noisy escape in the dilapidated truck.

Miles seemed especially anxious because it appeared that Elaine was focusing most of her attention his way. It didn't bode well.

Indeed, Elaine gave Miles a big grin. "I think you're about to be part of the chess competition, aren't you?"

Miles nodded. "That's the plan. Are you . . . playing chess, too?"

Jack was climbing one of the larger gnomes and Elaine held out a hand to help steady him. "I won't even be ready for the beginner level right now, but I'd love to go watch and learn. I'm really trying to ramp up. The cool thing about this hobby is it's very inexpensive and it doesn't have to take a lot of time. You know how crazy my life can be with Jack around. I always *think* I have all this time to learn a language or a new craft and then things tend to fall apart."

Myrtle carefully refrained from saying anything and just gave Elaine a sympathetic nod. She didn't really think lack of time or focus was Elaine's problem. Sadly, a general lack of talent appeared to be the underlying issue for most of the hobbies.

"But chess is different. I can play against a computer and not even make a move for hours, if I get busy. I can read about chess moves in books or online at my own pace. And it's incredibly inexpensive—there are really no set-up costs involved." Her face was flushed with excitement.

Miles swallowed, having the feeling he knew what might be coming. "That's all very true."

"Right? Anyway, now I finally think I'm ready to play with a human. I was trying to play with Red, but then this case came up and now he has no time at all. I wondered if maybe I could play a game with you, Miles."

Miles quickly said, "Myrtle is actually a wonderful chess player, herself."

Myrtle shot him a dirty look.

Elaine turned to Myrtle and said, "Oh, I didn't even think about the fact you could play, Myrtle."

"Miles is exaggerating my abilities," said Myrtle. "I don't even know the names of all the pieces."

"Don't let that fool you," said Miles dryly. "Not knowing the names of the pieces doesn't mean she won't beat you."

Elaine helped Jack jump off the gnome and watched as he trotted over to another. "How about if I play Miles first and then Myrtle next? That way I can get more experience in."

Miles nodded, although he looked disappointed. "True. And it's good playing with a variety of different players."

"I think it'll be great to observe at the tournament, too. Who knows, maybe I could even get Jack into the game after he gets a little older."

Myrtle said, "I'm sure he'd be an *amazing* chess player when he's bigger. My grandson is absolutely brilliant, you know."

Jack, at this point, was curiously gnawing on the hand of one of the gnomes. Elaine quickly redirected him. Then she said, "Well, thanks so much for this! Miles, I'll be in touch about starting our game. Would you like to set the board up at your place or mine?"

Miles carefully considered this point. If he set it up at his house, it would be quieter and the chaos of toys wouldn't distract him. But if they set up the board at Elaine's, he might be able to more easily escape and make an excuse to leave. "Maybe at your house?"

She beamed at him. "Done! I'll set it up on the dining room table since we just use it for holidays. Come over whenever you want."

Miles looked a little leery of the idea to just drop in at Elaine's to play chess. Myrtle said, "Maybe it would be better if you set up a time in advance. After all, Red is probably in and out at weird hours, isn't he?"

"True. How about tomorrow, then? Jack takes a nap around 1:00 . . . would that work out?"

Miles gave Elaine a small smile and said, "That sounds great, Elaine."

Myrtle smirked. Miles was always a gentleman. Sometimes, it didn't serve him well.

Elaine and Jack happily walked back to their house. Myrtle murmured, "Good luck tomorrow."

They walked back inside Myrtle's house. Miles said, "She couldn't be too awful if she's been playing on a computer."

"Oh, never underestimate how bad Elaine can be at a hobby. Besides, she might have the computer set on pre-novice level."

Miles frowned. "Is there even any such thing as pre-novice?"

"If there is, I'm sure Elaine has discovered it. You'll be fine. You can always come up with some sort of excuse to leave."

Miles looked uncomfortable. "I don't want to hurt her feelings though. It might look like I want to escape."

"But you *do* want to escape. Just start thinking about solid excuses now so whatever you use will sound plausible."

Miles crinkled his brow. "How long is Jack's nap?"

"I'm sad to say that Jack actually does have a very long nap in the afternoons. He stopped having morning naps so he has a single, huge nap at 1:00."

Miles looked morose.

Myrtle decided a distraction was in order. "Why don't we go inside and eat our leftover breakfast for lunch? We can even watch my recording of *Tomorrow's Promise* when we do."

Miles perked up a little. *Tomorrow's Promise* was the soap opera Myrtle and Miles watched. It had started out being *Myrtle's* soap opera, but then she'd gotten Miles hooked on the outlandish storylines and the unlikely characters.

Soon they were eating sausage, bacon, pancakes, and biscuits.

Miles frowned at the television screen. "What's going on with Hawthorne? I don't remember what he's doing in the hospital."

"Oh, sure you do. He was trying to keep his baby from being kidnapped by his ex-wife. It was pouring down rain and he was throwing himself desperately at her minivan and she ran him down."

"And he's on life support? Was she really driving that fast in the rainstorm?" Miles knit his brows.

"We have to suspend our disbelief, Miles. This isn't reality TV, you know. Remember how we had to accept the fact that Shawn was abducted by aliens for two weeks? It makes viewing much easier if we don't question things."

Miles seemed to accept this and they watched in silence for another fifteen minutes while they ate. Then Miles reached another stumbling block. "Ronan and Bethany spend a lot of time in a hotel."

"That's where they live," said Myrtle impatiently.

Miles stared at her. "They live in a hotel?"

"Some people do," said Myrtle.

"Only people on soap operas," muttered Miles. "There's not all that much room. And only one bathroom."

"It's a *tremendous* hotel room."

"Yes, but it would make for a small apartment. And it would cost a small fortune. It would make much more sense for them to just rent an apartment instead."

Myrtle said in a tight voice, "Perhaps you should write to the show and let Ronan and Bethany know that."

Miles considered this. "I could. And when I do, I'll also mention the fact that the show features far too many individuals being brainwashed. Half the people on the soap have been brainwashed at some point or another."

"Suspension of disbelief, Miles! It's very important." She reached out for the remote and turned off the television. "What's on your mind? You always enjoy watching *Tomorrow's Promise*."

Miles sighed. "Sorry. I think I'm just in a cranky mood."

"Well, that's most unlike you. Would it help if you went home and took a nap? Really, you need to shake this mood somehow."

Miles shook his head. "I'm not at all sure that a nap would help. When I've taken naps lately, I've ended up feeling really groggy when I wake up. I go through the rest of the day in a stupor."

Myrtle decided that explained a lot, but decided not to comment on the point. Instead, she tilted her head to one side. "We need a change of pace. Let's go ahead and set out to see Ezra."

Miles winced. "I'm not sure that's the panacea for my issues, Myrtle. We've had a very busy day already."

"Yes, but now we're doing something that's allegedly relaxing and it doesn't seem to be working. Instead, we'll hop back into action by speaking to our botanist friend about the poisoned pie. We'll work our brains a little bit. Then you'll probably be so exhausted that you'll go home, fall into bed, and sleep for twelve hours. You'll be a brand-new Miles."

Myrtle devoutly hoped he'd be a brand-new Miles. She wasn't much caring for this particular version of her friend on this particular afternoon.

"Okay. I suppose that makes sense in a weird way. We'll visit Ezra, if you're sure he won't mind having two people drop in on him for absolutely no reason at all."

Myrtle stood up and grabbed her purse. "I'm positive."

Chapter Six

Miles drove them over to Ezra's house, not far from downtown Bradley. It was a small house with a very large yard, very fitting for someone who was a botanist. Miles dawdled behind Myrtle as they set out down his front walk and she rang the doorbell.

The door opened and Ezra looked out a bit suspiciously. He relaxed when he saw Myrtle and Miles. "Well, hello, you two! What a pleasant surprise."

Myrtle smiled. "We thought we'd pop in for a little visit, Ezra. Are you in the middle of anything?"

"Not at all. Just making the rounds watering my plants. Come on inside while I finish up."

They followed Ezra inside. He was a thin man in his forties with a very intellectual manner. Despite the age difference and the fact Myrtle had taught him long ago, she almost considered him a contemporary due to the fact he was such an old soul. He was the kind of person who puttered around with his plants, gave talks at the library and garden club, and spouted interesting facts about things he'd read. It was how Miles had gotten ac-

56

quainted with him, too, being interested in a variety of arcane subjects.

Ezra's house was full of books. So full of books, in fact, that he'd run out of places to keep them. They were stacked in piles against the walls and, in many cases, had plants sitting on top of them as if they were makeshift tables. There were just as many plants as there were books and the plants all looked healthy, thriving, and happy.

He got them settled on the screen porch at the back of the house. The space was full of hanging plants and plants on the floor and tables. There was soft jazz music playing from a speaker. He beamed at them. "Now, let's see. I don't do the hosting thing very often, but I want to do it *right*. Can I get you both some coffee? Or I have water."

Then he trotted off for a few minutes after getting their answers and returned with a tray of waters and some store-bought cookies.

They were munching on the chocolate chip cookies when Ezra turned to Miles. "Are you going to take part in the chess tournament?"

Miles nodded. "I'm planning on it. Are you?"

"Absolutely. I always like playing with a variety of different people and this will give me the best chance to learn something new. I'm not in it to win, of course. I'm not *that* kind of chess player," he said with a chuckle. He turned his gaze on Myrtle. "And Miss Myrtle? I know exactly how good you are at chess."

She shook her head. "Maybe I'm decent at chess, but I'm afraid the interest isn't really there. I'll cheer on the two of you at a distance. I believe my daughter-in-law is going to be there, too. She's a novice and is trying to learn the ropes. She sounded pretty excited."

Miles looked anxious again at the thought of Elaine playing chess with him.

Ezra took a sip of water and gave Myrtle a thoughtful look. "As I recall, Miss Myrtle, chess isn't the only thing you're good at. I believe you're also an excellent investigative reporter."

Myrtle preened at this. Her crime stories in the paper were her most-favorite to write. However, Red and Sloan, the editor of the paper, often conspired to keep her writing a helpful hints column. She was glad to be recognized for her more-important journalistic efforts.

"Well, thank you, Ezra. That's very kind of you to say."

Ezra continued slowly, "So I'm wondering if this visit might also have something to do with the death of Luther Cobb."

Myrtle beamed at him. "An excellent deduction! Our visit is partly to do with that, yes. I was wondering if my son might have come by and had a conversation with you about Luther's death."

Ezra nodded solemnly. "He did. At first, I thought our conversation might simply be focused on the botanical aspects of Luther's demise. But then Red started asking questions that led me to believe he might consider me a suspect in his death."

Myrtle waved a dismissive hand at the thought of her son. "Red is prone to making wild assumptions, Ezra. Don't worry about it."

Ezra relaxed at Myrtle's pronouncement. "That's good. I realize it might seem a little suspicious that I happen to have the deadly plant in question in my greenhouse out back."

He gestured toward the building behind them. It was a good-sized structure and also seemed chockful of plants of every description.

Miles cleared his throat. "They've identified the plant that killed Luther, then?"

"That's right. Or rather, I suppose *I* did. Red and a Lt. Perkins brought me a photo of the pie in question. I recognized the lovely berries right away."

Myrtle suddenly recalled one of Ezra's talks she'd attended. "Nightshade?"

Ezra gave her a pleased look. "An excellent deduction of your own, Miss Myrtle. Yes, belladonna or deadly nightshade."

"I was at your very informative talk at garden club when you discussed the plant. I couldn't place the berries at first, but being with you has jogged my memory. I can't remember exactly what you said about the effects of consuming it, though. Except that it would be fatal, naturally."

Ezra chuckled. "You don't remember because I didn't discuss it. Tippy was already giving me an askance look for discussing poisons at all. I have the feeling she was devoutly hoping the topic would shift swiftly to marigolds. I decided talking about the effects of belladonna wouldn't be appropriate for a garden club luncheon full of ladies of a particular age."

Miles had a protective hand to his throat just thinking about nightshade.

"And those effects are?" asked Myrtle sweetly.

"Well, he wouldn't have felt well. My understanding is that he consumed a good amount of the pie. He'd have known fairly quickly that something was wrong—but with the hallucinations he might have experienced, it could have been tough for him to be lucid enough to call for help." Ezra paused. "His wife wasn't around?"

Myrtle said thoughtfully, "I got the impression that she was *around*, just not with Luther. She was in another part of the house or yard."

"Right. So he'd have also had a speedy heartbeat, possible mental incapacitation, and then a coma. It all would have happened fairly rapidly."

Miles said, "So he really *might* not have called for help."

Ezra shrugged. "Or maybe he called for help, but not very loudly."

"And you have belladonna here?" asked Myrtle.

Ezra nodded. "The police were very interested in it. Unfortunately, we came to the conclusion that some of my plants had been harvested. That likely made me seem even more suspect. It's actually rather late in the year for the berries to still be around, but the weather has remained unseasonably warm."

Miles knit his brows together. "Your greenhouse isn't locked?"

"Why would it be? No one has expressed an interest in it before. But I've made sure the yard is fenced in and inaccessible for any kids who might happen by. As I told Red, that was always my concern—that children might visit and come in contact with some of the poisonous plants. Preventing a *murderer* from accessing them was far from my mind. No one should be on my property," he finished indignantly.

Myrtle studied the fence. "I suppose someone could scale the fence, if they were determined."

"That was Red's conclusion, too. It's a six-foot fence, but anything would be possible with a small ladder. And my yard backs up to the woods, so it would be easy enough to do if you were motivated."

Miles said slowly, "I'm not sure I understand how a murderer would know about your belladonna. Or even be able to identify it."

"Oh, that's pretty easy. I had that recent talk—"Beer with a Botonist." He pushed his glasses up on his nose and looked a bit discouraged.

"I must have missed that one," said Miles.

Ezra smiled at him. "You should try coming to the next one. They're so much fun. I have a variety of beers and then talk plants."

"Surely, no matter how popular the talks were, there would be a limited number of people for Red to speak with, though. People who were interested in poisoning someone," said Myrtle.

Ezra gave her a rueful look. "Unfortunately, it was posted online. And it had lots of views. At least Red should have a lot of different suspects besides me."

"I can't imagine that you're a very serious suspect," said Myrtle. "Did you have an alibi at all? Anything to keep Red from investigating you much further?"

"Sadly, I don't have an alibi at all. I was at home, puttering around with my plants as per usual. I had no idea that I would need an alibi at all or I'd have been speaking to people at the grocery store or something. However! I think anyone would attest that I don't know how to bake. I might be able to manage cookies, but a pie would be completely outside my purview."

Miles said, "Myrtle has determined that the pie was store-bought."

Ezra slumped a bit at this. "That's a pity. I suppose anyone could have doctored a store-bought pie." He was quiet for a moment, in thought. "How much of this pie did Luther consume? He would have had to eat about ten or twelve of the berries for the poison to be fatal."

Myrtle pulled out her phone and opened the photo of the pie. She held it out for Ezra and Miles to see. "Unfortunately, we don't have a photo of the pie *after* Luther consumed it. But I'm supposing he must have eaten a good deal of it to have perished from in the manner he did."

Ezra asked, "May I see the photo up-close for a minute, Miss Myrtle?"

She handed her phone to him and he gently took it from her and studied it. "I see. So whoever the killer is took no chances. The pie is full of berries. Luther would have been scooping them out with every mouthful. That must have taken some time for the killer to doctor the purchased pie to that extent. They would have had to scoop out the original berries, added these, and then re-baked it with a new crust."

Ezra passed the phone back to Myrtle and Miles glanced at it as it went by. He said, "These berries—they must have tasted fairly sweet then? They're not bitter?"

Ezra gave him a wry look. "You'd think that nature would have ensured that something so dangerous would taste sour or bitter. But the berries from the deadly nightshade plant are very sweet. And, of course, they're attractive, too. They don't look like something that shouldn't be eaten. I'm sure Luther probably enjoyed every single bite."

Myrtle asked, "There's no way that the perpetrator intended the pie simply to be a warning, is there?"

Ezra shook his head. "It's pretty doubtful, considering the number of berries that were in the pie. I could see that if they'd just put a few berries in. But with this number, it seems certain that they planned for the recipient to die." He sighed. "And now I've got to look into locking up my greenhouse."

Myrtle tilted her head to one side and regarded Ezra thoughtfully. "It occurs to me that someone might have poisoned Luther to kill two birds with one stone."

Ezra raised his eyebrows. "I'm not sure I like where you're going with this, Miss Myrtle. Am I one of the two birds?"

Miles nodded. "It does make sense. Perhaps someone was unhappy with both Luther and with you. By poisoning and killing Luther, they'd rid themselves of him. But they'd also make *you* a prime suspect."

"Precisely," said Myrtle. She shot Miles an irritated look. She believed sidekicks should be seen and not heard.

Ezra looked a bit shaken. "Well, that's a pretty terrible thing to consider."

Myrtle said, "You know Miles and I think you're a wonderful person, Ezra. But are there people who might consider you an enemy?"

Ezra balked at the word. "I wouldn't think anyone would consider me an *enemy*."

"An adversary, then. Perhaps just a mild antagonist of some kind." Myrtle suppressed a sigh. Ezra could be entirely too focused on his plants and not as much on the world around him. And, maybe, people who didn't care for him and wanted to set him up.

He was quiet for a moment, taking a couple of sips of water as he considered the question. "Well, there's Olive."

"Olive? Is that Olive Fuller?"

Ezra looked leery. "Oh gosh. Is she a friend of yours? Please don't tell her I mentioned her."

"I certainly won't tell her anything of the sort! I'm very discreet," said Myrtle.

Miles gave her a dubious look at the mention of discretion.

"But you do know her?"

Myrtle said, "Olive Fuller is a member of my garden club. I'm not exactly her best friend. My main impression of her is that she is a very knowledgeable member and takes lots of notes during our meetings. If she showed up at one of your talks, I'm sure she might leave with reams of information about local poisons."

"Okay." Ezra still hesitated. "I can't imagine Olive would do something like this, though."

"Just tell us what your issue with Olive is and let *us* decide," said Myrtle.

"And this won't go into the newspaper?" asked Ezra, still stalling.

"Certainly not! I can't put hearsay in the newspaper. The paper would be sued and that would be the end of it."

"Okay," said Ezra again. He sighed. "The truth of the matter is that Olive is my neighbor. She and I have butted heads a few times over landscaping."

Miles frowned at this. "Landscaping," he repeated slowly, as if he couldn't picture a less-acrimonious subject.

"That's right. Oh, I know it sounds ridiculous."

"Not at all," said Myrtle breezily. "There have been plenty of days when I've wanted to kill my neighbor Erma over her invasive crabgrass."

Ezra looked relieved to hear this. "Well, in our case, it isn't crabgrass—it's a tree. Olive wants more sun in her backyard so she can better grow a variety of plants. I suppose she's heard about these plants during the garden club meetings. Anyway, she and I talk from time to time about native plants. Usually our conversations are very interesting. But when she wanted to cut down this lovely tree, I couldn't seem to help myself."

Myrtle said, "And Olive objected to this?"

"To the point she wanted to set you up to take the fall for a murder?" added Miles doubtfully.

"When you put it that way, it does sound rather silly," admitted Ezra. He spread out his hands. "But that's the only person I can think of that I had any sort of clash with recently."

Myrtle nodded and then stood up. "Thanks for this, Ezra, and for the cookies and drinks. Miles and I should probably head on out—we've had a long day."

"Still barely sleeping, Miss Myrtle? I don't know how you're always so alert during the day."

"Oh, I manage to collect some sleep here and there," said Myrtle with a shrug. "Maybe I'll sleep better tonight since I've been so active today."

"Hope so." He walked them both to the door and gave them a cheery wave as they left. "See you both later."

They got back into Miles's car and Miles headed off down the street. "Home?" There was that hopeful note in his voice again.

Myrtle shook her head. "Let's run by the newspaper office so I can discuss my story with Sloan."

"I presume you're *not* talking about this week's helpful hints column."

"Indeed I'm not. I'm talking about the piece I'll be writing about the mysterious circumstances surrounding Luther's death." Myrtle said this as if it was a fact.

Sloan, however, when they got there, appeared horrified. "Miss Myrtle, that's not a very good idea."

"No, it's an *excellent* idea," said Myrtle firmly.

Sloan shook his head. "If we had the police corroborate what you've told me, then that would be fine. But it sounds like we're going off of hearsay. A poisoned pie? It all sounds like trouble to me."

Myrtle produced the photo of the pie on her phone. "I do have a picture of the offending pie."

Sloan gingerly took the phone from her. He looked at the picture somewhat fearfully, as if the strange berries might leap out at him. He shook his head again. "We can't run it, Miss Myrtle. But what we can do is run a piece on Luther Cobb and mention all the facts that can be backed up. The time he was found, where he was, etc."

Myrtle had a confounded look on her face. Sloan didn't usually push back whatsoever. Even when Red sternly instructed him not to allow Myrtle to write crime stories, Sloan always capitulated whenever Myrtle announced she was going to write one.

Sloan said miserably, "Sorry. I have a bad feeling about this one. I think running a story without the police verifying the information would end up biting us."

Myrtle said, "All right. I'll see what I can do about getting the police to comment on the details of the crime."

Sloan and Miles both stared at her. Miles said, "Myrtle, Red won't give you any information."

"Then it's a good thing I'm such good friends with Lt. Perkins," she said with a smirk. She pulled out her phone and scrolled through her contacts. She rang his number, putting the call on speaker.

A moment later, he answered his phone. Myrtle said, "Ah, Perkins! It's Myrtle Clover."

Chapter Seven

To his credit, there was only a tinge of amusement in his voice. Apparently, she was the only octogenarian caller he received. "How can I help you, Mrs. Clover?"

"Here's the thing. I'm writing a story about Luther Cobb for the newspaper and I wanted to verify some of the facts about the case before the article ran. Is that something you can help me with?" asked Myrtle in her sweetest tone.

Perkins said politely, "I'd be happy to. Getting an accurate story in the press is always a good thing."

"Excellent," said Myrtle. "Could you verify that Luther died this morning? And do you have a particular time of death?"

"Luther Cobb did die this morning and the exact time is yet to be determined. I'd probably just go with 'morning.'"

Myrtle jotted down a couple of notes on one of the millions of pieces of paper that Sloan had in the newspaper office. "Got it. And would you say that his death was due to a poisonous pie?"

Perkins paused for a moment and then said, "I'd say that the cause of death is currently being investigated."

Myrtle made a face. "But you'd say that the cause of death appears suspicious."

Perkins considered this carefully. "I think that's fair to say. Let's word it this way: *Lieutenant Perkins with the SBI said the cause of death is currently being investigated, but foul play has not been ruled out.*"

"A very cautious way of putting it," said Myrtle. She couldn't help but admire the way he managed to say very little while making an official statement.

"Was there anything else?" he asked politely.

Myrtle could hear a good deal of noise in the background wherever Perkins was. She said, "I think that's it. Thanks for your time, Perkins."

"My pleasure, Mrs. Clover."

Myrtle hung up and turned to Sloan. "Will that work?"

He nodded, looking relieved. "Good work, Miss Myrtle. I don't often get official statements from the state police."

"It's all about connections," said Myrtle in a self-satisfied tone. "I'll write the story for you as soon as I get home so that it can run in tomorrow's paper."

Sloan looked a bit more cheerful at this and was whistling to himself as Miles and Myrtle left.

"Home?" Miles asked again.

"For heaven's sake, Miles! You're obsessed with being at home these days. Yes, let's head back. I've got to work on this story now. It might be good to take a big-picture view on what I need to do in the next few days, too. I do have garden club tomorrow." She looked thoughtful for a moment. "Maybe Wanda should come along with me. She hasn't been for a while and she does love plants."

Miles looked uncomfortable, as he always did when Wanda was brought up. It was a combination of Wanda's surprising psychic abilities, her aching poverty, and the fact that he was inexplicably a cousin of hers and her brother, Crazy Dan.

Myrtle gave him a sidelong look. "Maybe you should come along, too. Guests are always welcome at garden club."

"Sadly, I'm going to be playing chess during that time."

Myrtle chuckled. "Oh, that's *right*. You and Elaine."

Miles seemed eager to change the subject. "Back to Ezra. What did you make of what he was saying?"

"He sounded pretty truthful to me. But I have to wonder if he's being truthful with *himself*. After all, there's quite a possibility that someone killed Luther, using Ezra's plants, because they wanted to set him up. Surely, he must have some real enemies and not just Olive Fuller seeking revenge because Ezra didn't want her to chop down a tree."

Miles said, "But you know how neighbors can be. We've seen some of that before. Squabbling over things that seem very insignificant and end up becoming major feuds. Besides, Olive seems like the type of person who might get her feelings hurt easily."

"True." Myrtle mulled this over. "I think I should give Lucinda a call at some point."

"Lucinda?"

"She's a good friend of Ezra's. Actually, she was a close friend of his all the way back in high school. They were just like two peas in a pod."

Miles raised his eyebrows. "Non-dating peas?"

"That's correct. People say men and women can't be just-friends, but they're absolutely wrong. Look at us. We have no intention of dating each other."

Miles quickly agreed with this.

"Anyway, Lucinda might have more of a clear-headed view of who might possibly want to set Ezra up to take the fall for a murder. I should speak with her." Miles pulled into Myrtle's driveway and Myrtle added, "But not today. I think that was entirely enough for today. Plus, I need to write this story so it can get into tomorrow's paper."

"And, apparently, feed the cat." Miles gestured to Myrtle's front porch where Pasha sat, blinking at them.

"What a darling girl! Yes, I need to feed Pasha. If I do, it should also curtail some of her bloodthirstiness. There have been far too many 'presents' on my front step lately."

Miles shifted uncomfortably and looked squeamish. "Feed her well, then. See you later, Myrtle."

Myrtle went inside to feed a grateful Pasha and write an extraordinary article for the paper.

The next morning, Myrtle called Wanda bright and early. She was never sure if Wanda's house phone was operational (her brother was lackadaisical about paying bills), so she called the cheap cell phone that the newspaper had purchased for Wanda's benefit. Wanda, as a psychic, wrote the horoscopes for the paper. Most of the newspaper's subscribers, actually, could likely be attributed to Wanda's incredibly detailed predictions.

Wanda quickly answered, "Thought you might call."

"Good morning, Wanda! You might have known I was planning on calling even before I did. It must be very convenient to know what's going to happen in the future. Anyway, I wanted to consult you on a couple of different things. One of them we can discuss later. The other is a bit more pressing . . . would you like to attend garden club with me today?"

Wanda responded with alacrity again. "Yes."

"Oh, good. You always seem to get a lot out of the programs—more than I do, as a matter of fact." Wanda would *like* to take notes during the programs, but there was a problem of limited literacy. Wanda dictated her horoscopes to Myrtle and Myrtle sent them in to Sloan. Myrtle said, "We can do what we did last time and I can tape the lecture portion so you can listen to it later."

Wanda sounded pleased. "That sounds good, Myrtle."

"Now there's just the matter of getting you over here." Myrtle sighed. The vehicles at Wanda's house were often up on concrete blocks and completely non-operational. Myrtle had no vehicle at all, although she was always quick to point out that she had a valid driver's license. "I could perhaps borrow Miles's car."

Wanda said, "Dan kin drive me. His truck is workin'."

"Is it? What an unexpected surprise! Is he available to get you here fairly soon?"

There was a raspy chuckle on the other end of the line. "He ain't doin' nothin' so I reckon so." She paused. "Gotta figure out what to wear."

Myrtle said, "Yes, that's always a conundrum, isn't it? This club meeting is at Tippy's house, which makes it even worse."

"Got one of the outfits you gived me. Might wear that one."

Myrtle and Wanda had gone on a clothes shopping extravaganza at the second-hand store and picked up a variety of different garments for Wanda. It was a relief to hear that they weren't all in the hamper. "That would be great, Wanda. I'll see you soon, then."

About an hour later, Myrtle heard the sound of a very loud truck. It made Dusty's truck sound quiet in comparison. She quickly walked to her door and opened it. Sure enough, Crazy Dan, Wanda's brother, was at the wheel of the truck. He gave her a jaunty wave and Myrtle returned it. Wanda slipped out of the truck and made her way to Myrtle's front door. She was wearing black slacks and a black and white top. She gave Myrtle an uncertain, gap-toothed smile.

"You look absolutely perfect, Wanda," said Myrtle.

"My shoes aren't great," said Wanda, sticking out one of the offending items for Myrtle's review.

"Hmm. Perhaps they just need a little scrubbing?"

"Naw, I think they're just scuffed up to death."

Myrtle snapped her fingers. "I have an extra pair of black shoes you can wear. In fact, I was about to take them to the Goodwill. Would you like to try those? It looks like we wear the same size."

They did. Myrtle studied the results. "Well, they're in much better shape than yours. But you might be too young to wear orthopedic shoes."

Wanda looked pleased, though. "Them's comfortable."

"That's about all they have going for them."

Wanda still seemed amazed by them. "Think I could stand on my feet all day in them things."

"They're yours if you want them. You'll be able to try them out, anyway, because we're going to need to walk to Tippy's house. Ready?"

They set out down the road. Pasha, always enamored by Wanda, slipped out of some nearby bushes and joined along.

Myrtle beamed at her. "Brilliant Pasha! She's here to accompany us."

Wanda reached down to rub the cat and Pasha lifted her chin so Wanda could gently scratch underneath. They set out again—an octogenarian, a psychic, and a brilliant black cat.

Tippy lived in a large white home with columns and a large veranda. She was involved in just about everything in the town of Bradley—not just involved, but often running it. She was part of Myrtle's book club, as well. Myrtle hoped Tippy had finally given up on trying to recruit her into her different organizations. It wasn't Myrtle's idea of a fun retirement to be on a bunch of different committees or attending meetings every week.

Tippy greeted them at the door looking elegant as always in white slacks and a silky black top. "Good to see you both! Wanda, I was wondering when you might be able to make another meeting. Come on in and help yourselves to some food. We have so much here that I'm worried Benton and I are going to end up with all the leftovers."

Looking at the tremendous spread of food that Tippy had prepared, it did seem to be likely. There were little sandwiches of all different sorts with the crusts cut off. But there were warm foods, as well, in chaffing dishes: shrimp and vegetable skewers, meatballs, and mini quiches. It was as if they were attending a wedding reception instead of a garden club meeting.

Tippy fluttered off to greet some other guests and Myrtle said in a quiet voice to Wanda, "She's gone over-the-top with the food again. Get as much as you want. We might do well to find a plastic bag and stick some food in my purse for later. This crowd doesn't do much eating."

It was true. The garden club members liked oohing and ah-hing over the food, but very little of the victuals ever passed between their lips. Myrtle thought it was because the group spent too much time gossiping. Wanda looking longingly at the table of food but hesitated, seeming self-conscious.

Myrtle quickly walked over to the table, grabbed a plate, and heaped the food up high on it. She had the feeling that Wanda would feel uncomfortable holding such a plate, so glanced around for a good place to set it down. Fortunately, in Tippy's home, there was a variety of furniture just waiting for something to be put on it. Myrtle chose a tall table near the wall and a window.

They sidled up to the table and Wanda quickly ate. The only unfortunate part about their location was the fact that Erma Sherman, Myrtle's neighbor, was heading their way. Myrtle flinched, waiting for Erma to trap her there while she talked about whatever vile medical condition she had. She was greatly relieved to discover that Erma had a different target—Olive Fuller, a spindly woman who was looking around Tippy's fabulous home with discontent. Olive, of course, was someone who Myrtle wanted to speak with, as well, considering her squabble with Ezra over the tree in her yard.

Ordinarily, Olive was not the sort of person that Myrtle would seek out at garden club. She had an unhappy, dissatisfied face and had a belligerent manner when she spoke. She devoutly hoped that Erma would finish tormenting the woman soon and Myrtle would have her chance to ask her a few questions.

Myrtle noticed with satisfaction that Wanda had already quietly finished off half of the contents of the plate. Myrtle herself wasn't particularly hungry, so let her have the whole thing. She tried to tune out Erma's nasally voice, but it was like an earwig that wouldn't leave her alone.

"I guess you heard about your neighbor," Erma was saying to Olive. "Guess you must be feeling scared, living right next door to a murderer like that." She gave Olive a leering look.

Olive said dryly, "Absolutely nothing surprises me about Ezra Blake. Including murder."

Myrtle couldn't resist pushing her way into their conversation. In fact, she felt as if their conversation had bullied its way into her relaxing moment with Wanda, so she didn't feel bad about it whatsoever.

"Ezra Blake has more important things to do than poison people he doesn't even know," said Myrtle coldly.

Erma raised her bushy eyebrows. "Didn't realize you knew the man, Myrtle."

"I certainly do. I've known him most of his life. I taught him when he was a teenager. And he's my friend." Myrtle gave them a fierce look which seemed to cow Olive but had virtually no effect on Erma.

Erma said, "He does *too* know Luther Cobb. I've seen the two of them talking together."

"When?"

Erma shrugged. "Who even knows? I don't keep up with stuff like that. It was after one of Ezra's poison talks."

"Ezra doesn't hold 'poison talks.' He speaks about botanicals. Some of those botanicals happen to be poisonous. As a public service to our community, he explains which ones are so we won't go around accidentally poisoning ourselves."

This didn't seem to resonate with Erma, who was stuck on the idea of Ezra teaching poisoning. "Why, he even spoke here at garden club a couple of times."

"He did indeed," said Olive, giving Myrtle a look of dislike as if the entire Ezra Blake situation was her fault.

"Which was very good of him considering the fact that the club is full of a bunch of spiteful old biddies," said Myrtle with a sniff.

Perhaps fortunately, the meeting started at that very moment. Tippy called them all to order and they took their seats in various perches around the room. Myrtle waited until the dry part of the meeting, the minutes and so forth, were finished and then took out her phone and recorded the lecture, which was all about designing a sunny perennial garden. Wanda looked completely absorbed as the guest lecturer from the local extension service gave the talk.

After the lecturer finished up, everyone clapped and then started gossiping again. Myrtle glanced around for Olive. Although the woman had certainly irritated her, she still needed to speak with her about Ezra.

"Where did she go?" asked Myrtle with aggravation.

Wanda seemed to immediately know whom she was speaking of. She nodded across the room. "Over there with Blanche."

They walked over but Wanda didn't make it all the way to Olive and Blanche because she was beset upon by various garden club attendees who wanted to know their personal fortunes. Myrtle winced for her, but continued walking with determination over to Olive.

Olive gave her a frown as she joined them. That might have been because she was just saying to Blanche that Ezra must have killed Luther.

Myrtle pursed her lips and then said, "That's libelous, Olive."

"It's the truth, Myrtle. No one has nightshade in their gardens anymore. Only Ezra. And he's an odd man who keeps to himself."

Myrtle glowered at her. "He's an introvert, Olive. Many people are introverts and are completely harmless. Although, it occurs to me Olive, that you don't seem to care for your neighbor very much. Are you harboring a grudge against him?"

Olive sniffed. "And if I were?"

"Think about it. It's obvious that someone is trying to set up Ezra to take the fall for Luther's death. Like you said, hardly anyone grows nightshade anymore. Someone wanted to make it look as if Ezra murdered Luther. Considering your clear antipathy toward the man, it might have been you." Myrtle watched her coolly.

Blanche started chuckling. "Olive, did you really set up Ezra because of your tree situation?" With Blanche, you could never tell if she was joking or if she was serious. Blanche herself might not even have known.

Olive glared at Myrtle. "Of *course* I didn't kill Luther. Of *course* I didn't try to set Ezra up."

Myrtle said, "You don't sound particularly convincing. Do you have an alibi for Luther's death?"

"I don't even know when it happened!"

"In the morning. Where were you in the morning?" asked Myrtle.

"*When* in the morning?"

Myrtle said shortly, "*All* morning."

Blanche kept on chuckling, enjoying the exchange immensely.

Olive gave them both a furious look. "I was at home, rehabilitating a plant that another neighbor asked me to take care of. It's ailing."

"How charitable of you," said Myrtle dryly.

"I'm very proud that I'm able to help my neighbors with their problems. The plant wasn't doing well at all and now it's thriving. They're very relieved."

"I doubt that Red will think that's much of an alibi. Considering the fact that the plant isn't a sentient being."

"Red?" Olive was now looking alarmed.

"Yes, my darling baby boy and only child," said Myrtle fondly. "He's often misguided, however and tends to focus his energies in the wrong places. I'll be sure to redirect him since he doesn't appear to know about the Great Tree Issue that has created such antipathy between you and Ezra."

"Look, I don't know anything about Luther's death," said Olive hastily. "And, yes, Ezra has gotten on my nerves, but that's *it*. I surely wouldn't do anything to harm him."

"Even indirectly?" Myrtle quirked an eyebrow.

"Of course not!"

Myrtle gave her a considering look. "Well then, perhaps you'd better supply some other suspects. Because right now, you're looking fairly promising as a candidate."

Olive clearly enjoyed being an expert—whether it was on the subject of plants or determining suspects in a murder case. She took a thoughtful pose. "Funny you should ask that. I've been considering the topic, too. Since you're a friend of Ezra's, I presume you know about Lucinda."

"Lucinda has been Ezra's best friend since they were kids. I'm fairly certain she wouldn't be trying to set him up. Why not do it years ago, if she did? And what would be the motive?"

Olive looked cross. "No, no, I'm not suggesting anything like that. I've just noticed that Lucinda and Marshall seem to have an odd relationship. And Marshall doesn't seem to like Ezra at all."

The part about Marshall disliking Ezra made Myrtle prick up her ears. "Is that so? I guess I shouldn't be shocked, though—it must be hard for Marshall to accept that his wife has such a close relationship with Ezra."

Marshall Sanders was very different from Ezra. Either by accident or design, he looked quite a bit like a golf pro. Blond, tanned, and fit, he was just about the complete antithesis of academic Ezra.

Olive briefly looked concerned that she might have spoken out of turn. "Now, I'm not saying that Marshall would have wanted Ezra in trouble. Or that he killed Luther, mind you. I wouldn't want that kind of gossip to be circulating around on my behalf. I'm simply saying that I don't think Ezra and Marshall have the warmest relationship."

Myrtle said, "You also mentioned that Marshall and *Lucinda* have an odd relationship."

Olive now colored. "I might have spoken in haste. But it seems to me that Marshall isn't particularly warm toward Lucinda. I don't see the two of them holding hands and whatnot." She waved her hands dismissively. "Anyway, it was only an impression. Don't quote me on it."

For someone who liked to be in-the-know, Olive was apparently sensitive about spreading *mis*information. Myrtle supposed she had the sort of mother who likely frowned on gossip.

Myrtle said, "Well, it was good talking with you, Olive." Myrtle had the sort of mother who frowned on lying, however it seemed polite to give white ones from time to time. Olive didn't really notice Myrtle's defection from their conversation since someone else came up to speak with her.

Myrtle was about to rescue poor Wanda from a veritable gaggle of garden club members when she felt a tug at her elbow.

She turned and found, to her horror, that she was face-to-face with Erma Sherman.

Chapter Eight

Erma gave her a leering grin. "Can I be your sidekick again?"

Myrtle recoiled. Erma was decidedly *not* sidekick material. Sure she had, somewhat accidentally, helped with a couple of cases. But it was only in the most roundabout of ways.

Myrtle deftly skirted the question, instead, asking one of her own. "Does this mean you have information to share?"

"Course I do!" Erma gave her braying laugh and winked at Myrtle. "You know I always have my fingers on the pulse of the town."

Myrtle wouldn't have said that. She'd found that most everyone with a pulse in Bradley hastily headed in a different direction when Erma was heading their way. "What have you got?" she asked crisply.

Erma gave an elaborate pantomime of checking to make sure that Olive was otherwise occupied. Satisfied she was safely out of earshot, she leaned forward. Myrtle, naturally, leaned back. This, unfortunately, had the unsatisfactory result of making Myrtle off-balance. She stumbled backward and Erma grabbed her arm again to catch her.

"Steady there," said Erma with that braying laugh again.

Myrtle removed her arm and gave Erma an expectant look. "The information?"

Erma said, "I happen to know that the tree episode was a bigger deal than Olive was letting on."

"The tree in Olive's yard that she wished to cut down and that Ezra wanted her to keep?"

Erma chuckled. "The very one. Olive wants more sunlight in her backyard in order to grow stuff." Here, Erma seemed puzzled as to what exactly Olive might be wanting to grow. She shrugged. "Anyway, Ezra figured out Olive's plan because he saw a tree service truck outside. He marched right over there and told her she couldn't touch the tree—that it would be a *travesty*." Erma paused a moment, waiting for a reaction from Myrtle.

"Well, cutting down healthy trees *is* something of a travesty." She glanced across the room to where Wanda was apparently giving fortunes to the assembled garden club gals. Wanda gave her a weary look. "Get to the point, Erma."

Erma, luckily, sped up the story. "Anyway, that made Olive *furious*. She ended up yelling at Ezra. Apparently, she's not used to people telling her what to do. So Olive was red in the face, screaming. She even said some *bad words*." Erma's voice dipped precipitously as she gave a pious look.

Myrtle frowned. "How exactly are you getting the information for this fly-on-the-wall rendition of this story, Erma? I can't imagine that you were at Olive's house when this occurred."

Erma looked proud. "Clarabelle Martinsson is my friend and she lives directly next door to Olive. Plus, Clarabelle spends lots of time on her screened porch."

Plus, Clarabelle was an eavesdropper and gossip-monger. It all made sense now.

Erma apparently wasn't ready to stop being helpful. "There's more, too. It's not the first time Ezra has gotten involved with Olive's yard. She was getting her yardman to prune her crepe myrtle trees and Ezra came flying out saying the trees didn't need pruning too far back. Said it ruined the natural form of the tree. Olive really lost it. She doesn't like being told what to do."

"Well, thanks for this information, Erma," said Myrtle, starting to sidle away. "I need to collect Wanda now."

Or throw her a life preserver. The crowd around her was decidedly growing. She could hear Blanche asking Wanda if Blanche's current beau was "the one."

Myrtle inserted herself in the very middle of the crowd surrounding Wanda. This was easy to do because Myrtle wielded a cane and she wasn't above using it. The women, all of them younger than Myrtle, stepped carefully away from her. Myrtle said, "Ready?" to Wanda and Wanda gave her a relieved nod.

Myrtle sent Wanda on ahead while she made a quick visit to the table still piled with foods. The caterer for the meeting had tried to put a box of zipper bags in an inconspicuous location. Myrtle's eagle eyes spotted them, however. She hastily filled up several bags, stuffed them in her large pocketbook, and hurried to meet up with Wanda outside.

They made their way down Tippy's long, tree-lined driveway to the street.

"Sorry about all that foolishness," said Myrtle, scowling. "Those women lose their marbles when you're around."

"Sorry you got stuck with Erma," said Wanda, well-acquainted with Myrtle's struggles with her neighbor.

"Well, that's all par for the course. I hadn't had an Erma encounter for a long time. I guess all good things must come to an end."

"Suppose she told you about the tree," drawled Wanda.

"Yes, she did. And it saddens me that I apparently had a completely unnecessary conversation with Erma since it's clear you know all about the tree in dispute."

Wanda nodded. "Jest a little bit. I know Olive was real mad. Ezra was kinda sayin' he knew better than she did what to do with the tree."

"*Naturally* he did. He's a botanist. Olive is simply a know-it-all with a big mouth. I guess it all boils down to the fact that Olive was furious at Ezra. It doesn't even really matter what it was about. She was angry and she might have wanted to get back at him. Would Olive have chosen to murder Luther Cobb in order to implicate Ezra? That seems a bit farfetched, but then, *Olive* is a bit farfetched."

Wanda raised an eyebrow. "Miles is gonna pick us up, by the way."

"Is he? Having the sight really is helpful, Wanda, isn't it? And what excellent timing. I was getting rather tired of walking today. Plus, my handbag is extremely heavy from all the contraband hors d'oeuvres."

Sure enough, Miles pulled up right next to them in his Volvo.

"Garden club?" he asked laconically.

Myrtle nodded. "Can you give us a ride back to the house?"

Wanda and Myrtle clambered into the car and Miles set off.

"Have you run away from home?" asked Myrtle. "I thought you were supposed to be playing chess with my daughter-in-law right about now."

Miles looked gleeful. "We had to stop our game after about thirty minutes. Jack flat-out refused to take a nap. It was wonderful." He paused. "The funny thing is, right before Elaine put him down, I swear that Jack winked at me as if he were planning the whole thing."

Myrtle said, "I'm sure he did. Jack is positively brilliant. He probably saw your discomfort at playing chess with Elaine and decided to throw the afternoon into chaos to help you out."

"Chaos is the right word for it. I've never heard such a commotion in my life."

Wanda drawled, "How was the chess?"

Miles sighed. "I'm afraid it didn't go very well, but that could have been because Elaine was so distracted by Jack's fussing."

"Unlikely," said Myrtle. "You're being very generous, Miles. We've seen that there's rarely a hobby in which Elaine displays the slightest bit of talent."

"It was something of a disaster. She got the pieces mixed up and was moving the rook like a bishop at one point."

"The poor thing," said Myrtle.

"Then there were more-basic errors. She was moving the pawns too much at the beginning of the game and her king was exposed in the center." Miles's face was worried.

"You look like you're going to be having nightmares about this game tonight," said Myrtle. "You should just start taking her pieces and be done with it."

Miles pulled into Myrtle's driveway. "I don't think I can do that. I feel bad for her."

"You're far too charitable. You should feel bad for *yourself*. Besides, the sooner she realizes this isn't the hobby for her, the sooner she can try to croquet or something more innocuous."

"I thought *chess* was innocuous," said Miles.

"Not in Elaine's hands, it's not."

They got out of the car and headed inside. "What's the plan now?" asked Miles.

"We regroup. I need to figure out what our next move is."

Miles asked, "How was garden club?"

Wanda croaked, "Program was good."

"And the food was good," added Myrtle, taking the zipper bags from her purse and putting them in the fridge. "But that's to be expected when Tippy is hosting. Poor Wanda was overrun by old biddies trying to get their fortunes, of course."

Poor Wanda shrugged a thin shoulder. "It was okay."

They settled into the living room.

"Did you find out any additional information about the case?" asked Miles.

"I did spend some time speaking with Olive. And an unfortunate amount of time speaking with Erma who is campaigning to be considered a sidekick."

Miles gave her a sympathetic look. "Sorry."

"Yes. At least she was able to offer a bit of information about Olive and Ezra. Apparently, the contretemps with Ezra over the tree was somewhat heated."

"*Can* a contretemps be heated?" Miles frowned.

"It cannot. It graduates to a dispute. Or perhaps an altercation. We were led to believe that it was a minor quarrel, but according to Erma, it was actually more than that. Plus, there was another issue over Olive's crepe myrtles."

Miles mulled this over. "So you're saying that Olive was so upset by Ezra's defense of the tree that she killed Luther and set Ezra up to take the blame?"

"I'm certainly not saying anything of the sort. But it's true that Olive deliberately downplayed the incident for one reason or another." Myrtle turned to Wanda. "What's your take on this?"

Wanda drawled, "Olive could've done it."

"That's what I think, too. I'm not *saying* she did, and it seems utterly implausible, but then Olive herself is utterly implausible. She likes to know things and she likes to be right. Maybe she just snapped. She must have known she wouldn't seem like much of a suspect. Olive could have felt sure she would get away with it."

Miles said, "Did Olive offer any information about who might have killed Luther?"

Myrtle pursed her lips. "She thought that there were all sorts of odd relationships going on around her. For someone who's never been married, she seems to believe she's very perceptive about relationships."

"Relationships? Was Luther having an affair?"

Myrtle said, "Who knows? Olive was more focused on the relationship between Marshall Sanders and his wife Lucinda."

"Lucinda, Ezra's best friend?"

"Naturally. How many Lucindas do you know? At any rate, she thought Marshall and Lucinda's marriage was rather odd. She intimated that either there might be something going on between Lucinda and Ezra or that Marshall *thought* there was."

Wanda croaked, "Ain't no relationship there. Just friends."

"Precisely. I've observed Ezra and Lucinda's friendship for decades and there appears to be no spark there whatsoever. They're just good friends who have a lot in common." Myrtle looked thoughtful. "I believe the next step is speaking to Marshall Sanders."

Miles raised his eyebrows. "You just said that Marshall didn't have anything to be jealous about."

"He doesn't. But human beings aren't rational. He might *think* he has something to be jealous about. That gives him a motive to try and set Ezra up for Luther's murder."

Miles said, "I still don't understand why Marshall would want to kill Luther, specifically, though, even if he were trying to set up Ezra."

Myrtle waved her hands around. "Maybe it didn't matter to Marshall *who* he killed. Maybe he was so focused on getting rid of Ezra for good that he was just looking for an easy target. And Luther *was* an easy target. He was recovering from a fairly devastating accident. Besides, lots of people were dropping off food for Dinah and him so it wouldn't look suspicious if he dropped off a pie laced with nightshade. It was just a crime of opportunity. We should pay him a visit."

Miles suddenly looked very tired. "We're not just going to walk over there and interview him at his house, are we?"

"Of course not. We'll go over to the high school where he works and speak with him there."

Miles's face was positively horrified.

Myrtle waved her hand dismissively. "It won't be that big of a deal, Miles. He not only teaches there, he coaches over there, too. We can walk the track by the school and wait for an opportunity to talk to him."

Miles looked down at his button-down shirt and khakis. "I don't think I'm properly attired for walking on a track."

"We won't be *jogging*, Miles. It's just the same as walking down the sidewalk."

"I think expectations are higher when one is walking on a track. There's a certain level of athleticism that's assumed."

"Not from people our age."

Miles looked unhappy at being looped in with Myrtle's age group. He was in his 70s and rather proud of it.

Myrtle turned to Wanda. "Would you like to walk around the track with us?"

Wanda, at the moment, was looking longingly at the deck of cards on Myrtle's kitchen table. She said slowly, "Can make it if you want me to."

Myrtle caught the longing look and said, "You've already had an exhausting day, what with the garden club gals. Why don't you settle down, turn on the TV, and play cards for a while? There's food from Tippy's house in the fridge. You still enjoy solitaire?"

Wanda nodded. "Wouldn't mind learning chess. Don't know if Dan'll play it with me, though."

Myrtle prided herself on her imagination, but still couldn't visualize Crazy Dan with his chewing tobacco and wild eyes being erudite enough to grasp, much less play, the game of chess.

Miles, who always felt a sense of responsibility toward Wanda said slowly, "I suppose I could teach you to play. It's the sort of game you can play with a computer pretty easily."

Myrtle quirked an eyebrow at him. "If one has a computer."

"Right." Miles colored. "I suppose you and I could have an ongoing game, Wanda. If you end up liking chess."

Wanda looked pleased. "Sounds good."

A few minutes later, Myrtle and Miles set out to his car and drove to the high school.

As Miles parked near the track and football field, Myrtle smiled, "Makes me feel like I'm back teaching school again."

"Do you miss it? Teaching, I mean?"

"Gracious no. I miss the *kids*, though. The kids always made it worthwhile. But I don't miss staff meetings and I certainly don't miss grading papers. When you're an English teacher, there are *lots* of papers to grade."

Miles winced. "I can only imagine."

"You must be feeling relieved that there was no grading involved in being an attorney. Although I suppose there was plenty of writing to do."

Miles gritted his teeth. "Engineer."

"Whatever," said Myrtle airily as she climbed out of the car.

They were faced with a good number of steps leading down through the stadium to the track. Miles gave them an uncertain look. "Are you sure you want to navigate those stairs? Going down will be easier than going up."

"Actually, when one has a tricky knee, it's easier going *up* than going down. Anyway, I'm going to hold on very carefully to your arm with one hand and my trusty cane with the other."

Miles frowned down at the people below. There were various teams doing warm-ups on the field and others who were running around the track. "Are we absolutely sure that Marshall is down there? I'm supposing he's very busy, too, if he's coaching."

"Pfft. Coaching has built-in breaks. You tell the kids to do however many pushups and then they have to spend time doing them. And he's down there . . . see the man with the blond hair and the golf shirt?"

Miles nodded and looked unhappily at the stairs again. "All right."

They made their way slowly down the stairs. They hadn't gotten but halfway down when suddenly, the blond man in the golf shirt bounded up the stairs toward them. "Miss Myrtle!" he called out. "Need some help?"

Miles muttered under his breath, "As if I weren't even here helping you. I feel very invisible right now."

"Be nice, Miles. He's something of an over-achiever. I guess helping little old ladies down stadium stairs makes him feel good about himself."

Miles cast a disbelieving glance over Myrtle. She was nearly six feet tall, quite sturdily-built, and didn't fit anyone's definition of a little old lady.

She called out to Marshall, "Thank you!"

Marshall was next to them in seconds and relieved Miles of his duties. "Are you just here to get a little exercise in, Miss Myrtle? I don't think I've seen you out here."

"Oh, my doctor is something of a fussbudget and he suggested I work out my knee a bit. I thought the track might be a good idea."

Marshall looked doubtful. "Is it? I'd think walking around downtown might be a little better. Going up and down these stairs might provide more of a workout than the doctor was expecting. Plus, you'll have members of the track team flying by you. Things could get dangerous."

"It'll be just fine, don't worry. Then I'll be absolutely worn out for the day and might be able to sleep tonight."

Marshall raised his eyebrows. "I seem to remember you talking in class about how you were an insomniac. Has that changed?"

Miles snorted as he made his way down the stairs behind him.

Myrtle turned to shoot him a look. She said to Marshall, "What an excellent memory you have! No, I'm afraid my sleeping hasn't much improved. At this point, I've simply given in to the insomnia. I'll get up and do laundry or go for a walk. It's much better than lying in bed and trying to count sheep and that sort of nonsense."

Marshall delivered her carefully to the bottom of the stairs and made sure she was standing steadily on the track before letting her go. He glanced back at Miles and said, "How are you doing there? All good?"

Miles was clearly trying to hide his irritation. Rather unsuccessfully, it turned out. "I'm good—I have no problems with stairs."

"That's good," said Marshall absently as he glanced across the field at his team. He suddenly bellowed at them, making Miles jump. "Hey! Who said you guys could stop? Single-leg squats, right *now*!" He turned back to them apologetically. "Sorry. My team will use any excuse to get out of exercising. Now, how are you doing, Miss Myrtle?" He turned to Miles. "Miss Myrtle tried to get me better at my native tongue many years ago when I was in high school. I do believe she was the only teacher able to make some headway. I was pretty stubborn back then, but she was able to get me to write a decent sentence."

Myrtle straightened her shoulders a little and looked pleased. "Why thank you, Marshall. That's so kind of you to say so."

"I won't much thank you for making me read that story about the poor pony, though." His face darkened. "Think I still have nightmares about that."

Myrtle raised her eyebrows. "*The Red Pony*? One of John Steinbeck's many masterpieces."

"And long." Marshall gave Miles a long-suffering look as if expecting sympathy. Miles, however, was quite the fan of Steinbeck and was still annoyed at Marshall, so he was only able to give him a tight smile in return.

"Long!" Myrtle snorted. "It's a novella. It was originally released in episodic form in a periodical."

"There you go speaking High English again," chuckled Marshall. "You've lost me."

"Anyway, it's fortuitous that I've run into you today. I've been thinking about you recently."

"Have you? Uh-oh. That sounds a little ominous."

Myrtle folded her hands together on top of her cane. "It's all this business with Luther Cobb."

Marshall nodded, glancing over at his team again. "One sec, Miss Myrtle." Then he hollered, "Okay, guys. Let's start doing burpees."

Myrtle and Miles looked rather alarmed as if something coarse and unseemly was about to unfold. They were relieved to see the team members do pushups followed by leaps into the air before squatting.

Marshall said, "Sorry, you were saying something, Miss Myrtle."

Myrtle repeated, "Luther Cobb."

"Ah, yes. I believe he just recently died, didn't he? That seems like bad luck. Wasn't the guy just recovering from a car accident?"

"That's right. Although his death didn't result from an accident."

Marshall raised his eyebrows. "You're not saying he was murdered?"

"I'm afraid he was. He was murdered."

Marshall blinked in surprise. "Wow. Well, that's very surprising. I mean, Luther wasn't the most popular man in town, but I can't imagine anyone wanting to bump him off. Was he shot or something?"

"He was poisoned. And I'm surprised, in a town like this, that you don't know anything about it. I'd have thought Lucinda would have filled you in . . . or any number of people."

Marshall shrugged. "Lucinda and I have been focused on other things, I guess. And aside from teaching and coaching, I haven't been out of the house much recently. The kids don't really care about stuff like that, you know."

Myrtle, actually, *didn't* know this. In her experience, her high school students had always had something of a macabre interest in local crime stories. But she said, "I suppose not."

Marshall said, "Poisoned. That's so unreal."

"Were you friends with Luther?" asked Miles politely.

Marshall shook his head. "No, I really didn't know the guy. I've heard people talk about him, though, and I've seen him out in public before. Kind of brusque, not real friendly."

"That sums him up pretty well," said Myrtle.

"Where was his house?" asked Marshall.

Myrtle told him and Marshall grunted again. "Too bad. I thought maybe I'd driven by it on my way to work or something. But I didn't, so I can't give any sort of information to the police. I'm sure they're not thinking his *wife* did it, are they?"

Myrtle was quite sure that the police *were* thinking that. It was so often the spouse when these types of things happened. But she said, "You know Red doesn't give me any information at all. He tends to keep his investigations to himself. Are you a friend of Dinah's?"

Marshall colored a little. To cover this, he turned toward his team again. "Water break!" he roared, making Miles jump. Marshall turned back toward them, seeming a bit more composed. "No, I don't know either one of them. It's just that it's hard to imagine a wife poisoning her husband, isn't it? It somehow seems like more of an outside job."

Myrtle was quite sure that poisonings were a preferred murder method by women. She found it very interesting that Marshall was defending Luther's wife. "Who do you think might have done it? Have you heard of anyone who was upset with Luther?"

He said hastily, "No, like I said, I haven't been out much aside from the school. And I didn't know Luther. It could have been anyone, couldn't it? He didn't have the best reputation around town, like I said. I don't think he was a really sterling guy, as far as I can tell."

Myrtle was tiring of Marshall's implausible vagaries. She said in a stern, schoolteacher voice, "Now, Marshall. You've lived in this town for too long not to know about the rumor mill."

Marshall tensed up. "Are people saying things?"

Myrtle said, "They are. About Jasper, as a matter of fact. I figured you might have a good take on it all, considering how involved he is over here. I believe he even does some coaching, doesn't he?"

Marshall nodded. "I didn't want anyone to think Jasper might have done this, but it sounds like word might already be out. Now, I don't think Jasper could hurt a fly, Miss Myrtle. But he did tell me that his son Archie had a run-in with Luther."

"What sort of run-in was it?" Marshall hesitated and Myrtle pursed her lips. "Apparently, there was some sort of minor incident involving vandalism that Luther was privy to? From what

I understand, Luther saw Archie do something untoward and threatened to report him to the authorities?"

"Well, I'm sure it was all really nothing. You know how boys are, Miss Myrtle. Well, I guess you must, since Red's your son."

"That's true. And Red was not always the most exemplary teenager. I found it rather surprising that he ended up devoting his life to crime-fighting. I hear that Archie is working very hard to get an athletic scholarship, is that true?"

Marshall nodded. "Yes, Archie has a real promising future ahead of him with baseball. There are always scouts showing up for practice to see what he's up to. I'm thinking he might end up going to one of the top schools in the country. He's the star of the team. Actually, he's probably the star of the *school*, across all of the different sports. Archie is a standout and I'm sure he's got a really bright future, like I was saying."

"If he doesn't have a checkered past," said Myrtle.

"Look, Miss Myrtle, all I know is that Archie didn't have anything to do with this guy's death. He was at an away game and even had to leave early and skip school to ride on the team bus."

Miles said slowly, "But you weren't with them? I thought you were the coach?"

Marshall shook his head and gestured to the kids on the field who were enjoying their extended water break. "I coach soccer; there's another teacher who coaches baseball. Like I said, I was just teaching that day."

Myrtle said cheerfully, "On a more pleasant subject, how is dear Lucinda doing? I haven't seen her for a little while."

Marshall said in a vague tone, "Oh, she's doing fine, Miss Myrtle. I need to probably take her out to dinner or something because I haven't seen much of her, myself. Between school and coaching and games, I haven't been around as much as I'd like."

"It's good she has such a nice friendship with Ezra," said Myrtle innocently. "Those two have always been peas in a pod since they were here in high school, themselves."

Miles looked anxious at this particular line of questioning.

Marshall suddenly appeared less vague and distracted and much more focused. "Yes. They always have been, haven't they?"

"I think you're such an understanding husband, really. Not many people understand that a man and a woman *can* be just friends. Miles and I are just friends for instance."

Miles gave Marshall a tight smile as if still concerned Marshall might suddenly snap at the mention of his wife and the botanist together.

But Marshall merely said, "Yes. And it's good that Lucinda has someone to talk to when I'm away so much." He paused. "You're probably away and busy quite a bit yourself, Miss Myrtle, aren't you? You're still working at the newspaper, right?"

It seemed to Myrtle like quite an abrupt change in conversation. Myrtle nodded. "That's right."

Marshall turned to Miles. "Miss Myrtle was in charge of the student newspaper when I was in school here. And the yearbook, I think?"

Myrtle nodded again. "And the literary magazine, as well. There was always something to do. But then, you understand that, too, since you teach and coach."

Marshall glanced at his watch. "Speaking of coaching, I've got to get back to it. Are you two going to be okay going back up the stairs?"

Miles bristled a bit. Myrtle said with a smile, "We'll be just fine, Marshall. Good to see you."

Marshall hurried away, looking relieved to be escaping their conversation. Miles sighed. "I suppose we have to walk, then? For appearance's sake?"

"For health's sake, too. We don't have much else to do today anyway, aside from your teaching Wanda how to play chess. We can walk for a little while, head back to my house for lunch, and then you and Wanda can play the game."

Chapter Nine

They started out along the track. Miles said, "It's a little discouraging seeing teen athletes zipping along next to us. It's sort of like a before-and-after video."

"Just remember that we were zipping along like that ourselves just decades ago," said Myrtle with a sniff.

"I'm not certain that I was ever that zippy."

"Let's focus on something cerebral instead, Miles. That's where we excel. What do you think about what Marshall told us?"

Miles considered this. "Well, he was certainly not being very forthcoming. He wasn't going to mention anything about Jasper or Archie until you brought it up."

"I had the feeling it was total nonsense that he didn't know anything about it. Archie is the school's star athlete and Jasper is a fellow coach at the school."

"You handled it very well."

Myrtle shrugged. "He's not that much different than he was when I taught him in school. He had the propensity to be somewhat shifty. You know—he'd claim that the dog consumed his homework. That sort of thing."

"But the dog hadn't?"

"One time I made him empty out his backpack and there was a completely untouched English handout in there. In fact, there were *multiple* English handouts. It was most aggravating. I'd spent a good deal of time at the mimeograph machine making those copies."

"He didn't seem to spend much time talking about Lucinda," noted Miles. "I think Olive might have been right about Lucinda and Marshall not having the fondest of marriages."

"And we'll need to speak with Lucinda. I'm afraid that I've become somewhat distracted today and led in different directions. Maybe we can visit with Lucinda after lunch. And chess."

Miles sighed. It was beginning to look like a very long and lively afternoon.

After their walk on the track (Marshall had assigned a young man to help Myrtle up the stadium steps and one who watched Miles like a hawk), Miles drove them back to Myrtle's house to meet up again with Wanda. They were all eating peanut butter and jelly sandwiches when Wanda suddenly paused. "Company's comin'."

Myrtle beamed at her. "This is so very convenient! I love knowing when people are about to show up at my doorstep. Are you able to see who it is?"

Wanda washed down a bite of her sandwich with her glass of milk. "That Lucinda. Comin' to see what's going on."

"Isn't that *perfect*? We were going to have to pay her a visit after chess this afternoon. And now she's on her way here. That's marvelous."

Myrtle quickly finished up her sandwich, ate a couple of cheese crackers, drank her milk, and then put her things away in the dishwasher. By the time she'd finished, there was a light tap at the door.

Myrtle peered out the side window (it never hurt to be cautious at her age) and saw Lucinda outside. "Just as you said, Wanda." She pulled open the door.

Lucinda looked at her a bit bashfully. "Hi, Miss Myrtle. I hope you don't mind the intrusion." She looked past Myrtle into the house and quickly said, "Oh no, you have company."

"This isn't company; it's just Miles and Wanda. Come on in, my dear. Can I get you a sandwich? We're just finishing up peanut butter and jelly."

Lucinda shook her head. "No thanks, I just ate."

She stood there on the front step looking hesitant and conflicted. Her brown hair which was streaked with gray looked a bit lackluster and her face was tired.

Myrtle steered her inside and to her recliner. "Heavens, Lucinda, you don't look at all well. Would you like a small glass of sherry?"

Lucinda looked as if she was about to turn down the offer but then hesitated. "If you'll have one with me, Miss Myrtle. Or Miles and Wanda?"

Miles and Wanda turned it down, so Myrtle quickly poured two drinks into her tiny crystal sherry glasses that had been her mother's. She gave Lucinda one and watched as Lucinda downed it as if it were a shot. Perhaps Lucinda thought it *was* a shot.

Myrtle gave small sips of her sherry as she watched the color return to Lucinda's face. "There now. Better?"

Lucinda gave her a grateful smile. "I think so. Thank you."

Since Lucinda still seemed at a loss for words, Myrtle decided the time had come to prompt her a bit. "Now, I'm thinking you must be paying me a visit for a very good reason, as delightful as it is to see you. Perhaps you're here because of Luther's death? And Ezra or Marshall being implicated in it?"

Lucinda looked alarmed. "Are they both suspects?"

"I think they must be, dear, don't you? But that doesn't mean they're the *best* suspects. There are plenty of others."

Miles and Wanda put their plates and glasses away and quietly joined them in the living room.

Lucinda looked down at her hands and picked at a nail. "Yes, I'm sure you're right. That's why I'm here, as you said. I wanted to find out if you'd spoken with Red and knew anything." She looked up, giving Myrtle a hopeful look.

Myrtle gave her a sad one in return. "Now, you know what I have to deal with when it comes to Red. He doesn't give me a lot of information."

"Is that what all the gnomes are out in the yard for?" asked Lucinda.

"That, actually, was for a different transgression. There are so many, it's a wonder that my gnomes aren't camped out in the yard all the time. But, sadly, I don't really have that much information about Luther's death."

Lucinda nodded but looked slightly deflated. "I've been so worried about Ezra through this whole thing. I just know Red thinks he's a suspect."

Myrtle said archly, "Red has been known to be wrong. Many times. I do indeed think Ezra is considered a suspect, however."

"But Ezra didn't really even *know* Luther. The only reason anyone thinks he's a suspect is because he has access to night-shade. Ezra is such a sensitive soul—it's just astounding that any-one could think he could murder someone."

"Yes, well, Red can be rather astounding sometimes," said Myrtle in a placid voice.

Lucinda continued, "He would never even hurt a living *thing*. He had this passionate argument with Olive over this tree she wanted to cut down. He just doesn't like to see anything killed. And he's being so responsible with all this; he even bought a tremendous padlock and has locked up his green-house."

Myrtle nodded idly, thinking that it was very interesting that Lucinda appeared to be so much more interested in defend-ing her friend Ezra than she was in defending her husband, Mar-shall.

Lucinda looked earnestly at Myrtle. "If you could, put in a good word for Ezra, would you? I really appreciate it."

"Of course I will, my dear. Ezra is a friend of mine, too. As are you. And, as a friend, I'm sure you'll understand if I feel the need to ask you about Marshall's interactions with Ezra."

Lucinda became very still.

Myrtle said, "Do you think it's possible that Marshall could be very jealous over your relationship with Ezra?"

Lucinda looked taken-aback by this.

"I don't think so, Miss Myrtle. I mean, Ezra and I have been friends for a very long time. It's not as if it's something new. Marshall isn't even around enough to really register how much time I spend with Ezra." The last was said in a tone of some bitterness.

Myrtle said, "I just wondered. I have the most fanciful things cross my mind sometimes, my dear, and it just occurred to me that Marshall could have been trying to set Ezra up for Luther's murder."

Lucinda automatically shook her head at this. "No way. I'm sure Marshall would never have done such a thing. Lots of people could have gotten into Ezra's greenhouse. It would have been easy to do while he was giving a talk or something. They'd have known he was out and they could have scaled the fence and just nabbed whatever they needed."

"Like Jasper Hodges, for instance?"

Lucinda blinked at the change of direction.

Myrtle said, "I'm not at all sure that Red knows anything about it, of course, although Bradley is such a small town that word might spread soon. But my understanding is that Jasper might have had some sort of contretemps with Luther over an incident with his son, Archie."

Wanda and Miles had been sitting very quietly and listening. But Wanda suddenly said in a sympathetic tone, "Poor Archie."

Lucinda's eyes filled with tears at the kindness in Wanda's voice and she swiped them away quickly. "Yes, I feel badly for Archie, too. Marshall talks about him a lot because he's so involved in the athletic program at the high school. Of course, I'll sometimes go with Marshall to the baseball games and watch Archie play, and I agree that he is an amazing athlete. Marshall's been very impressed with him. Everyone is acting as if Archie is so blessed with talent that he couldn't possibly have any problems. But the fact that he *has* talent and promise is what's making Archie's life so difficult."

Myrtle said, "I suppose there are many practices, aren't there? And probably training going on in addition to the practices?"

"Exactly. I've felt terrible for Archie because I keep thinking all he wants is just a quiet, typical teenage existence. He's never known what it's like to sleep until noon." She snorted. "He's never known what it's like to sleep until *eight*, not unless he was in bed sick with something. There are practices, at-home games, away games, long trips on buses, early and late nights working out, and lots of serious talks about school."

"Does Jasper feel bad for Archie, do you think? I'm sure you spend time with Jasper, too, considering he and Marshall work together in the athletic department." Myrtle tilted her head slightly to one side when she looked at Lucinda.

"I'm sure he does," said Lucinda quickly. "But Jasper wants the best for Archie—everyone at the school does."

Myrtle said, "But Jasper has certain expectations for Archie? I'd imagine those might create some additional pressure for a young man who wants to please his father."

"That's right. But it's just because he's invested a lot of time and money into Archie. And love, of course. He just wants Archie to have a good, successful future."

Wanda croaked again. "But Archie wants to have fun."

Lucinda didn't seem surprised at this insight. But then, she likely read Wanda's perceptive horoscopes like the rest of the town. "He does. That's only natural, isn't it? He wants to hang out with his friends, meet girls, and yes—get into trouble. Which he did, I guess. Or he *could* have. It was the trouble that Jasper was worried about. Archie has a couple of new friends, according to Marshall, and I suspect they aren't the greatest influence on him." She made a face.

"They're not athletes?" asked Miles.

"Right. So they just have school and homework and that's it. From what I've seen, they have the opposite problem—they have too *much* time on their hands. One day, they just decided to buy some paint and spray paint graffiti on a downtown building. One of them is eighteen and was old enough to buy it." Lucinda briefly put her head in her hands. "Stupid. Jasper and the other kids' parents made them go over there and clean it all up as soon as they realized what happened. It took them a lot longer to clean it up than it did to mess it up. Anyway, I guess they thought they'd gotten away with their crime because no one drove or walked by. They *thought*."

"Except for Luther," said Myrtle.

"I don't even know if he technically saw them doing it or if he just put two and two together when he saw them speeding away and then saw the paint on the building. Whichever it was, he made a good show of acting like he was positive they were guilty. I'm certain Archie has been scared straight now. Marshall said he was walking around like a ghost at the school. And he hasn't seen those new friends of his since. He seems to be over those friends and over rebelling or whatever it was that he was doing when he decided to vandalize a building. Even if he *did* get caught, I'm sure it probably would have counted as a misdemeanor." Lucinda shrugged. "To me, it was almost like a cry for help. The poor kid has been working so hard on school and sports that he just couldn't handle it anymore."

Myrtle nodded. "Honestly, since he helped clean it up, I have the feeling Red would have just let him off with a warning. There likely wouldn't have been anything on his record at all. Red was young once, himself, and far from perfect as a teenager. I'm sure he'd have understood."

Myrtle said, "I'm guessing that Luther's accusations didn't go over too well with Jasper."

Lucinda made a face and shook her head. "Not at all. He was horrified and then furious. But I'm sure he didn't hurt Luther. Poisoning someone seems pretty passive-aggressive. Jasper, on the other hand, is outright aggressive. He'd rather have out and out warfare than do something underhanded. It's just not the way he handles conflict. And Archie was out of town, of course, at an away-game. But Marshall said that Jasper was sure that it was all the beginning of the end. That Archie was going to somehow go from being the perfect collegiate prospect to being some washed-up kid working as a grocery store bagger for the rest of his life. It was like all his hopes and dreams were invested in Archie."

Wanda croaked, "The boy is gonna be just fine."

Lucinda nodded her head, satisfied. "That's exactly what I thought." She stood up and gave them all a smile. "Now I'm going to let you get back to your day. Thanks for letting me crash your party here."

Myrtle walked her to the door, and then returned to sit with Miles and Wanda. "Was it me, or did Lucinda seem a lot more concerned about her friend Ezra than she did about her husband Marshall?"

Miles said, "It was very clear."

Wanda drawled, "But she and Ezra ain't a couple. Jest friends."

Myrtle gave Wanda a smile. "Thanks for clarifying that. I wasn't at all sure that was still the case. Of course, Marshall might not believe that Ezra's and Lucinda's relationship is purely friendly."

Miles said thoughtfully, "I wonder if she was unconcerned about Marshall because she just can't believe that he would murder Luther. Lucinda sounded convinced that he didn't have anything to do with it."

Wanda suggested, "She's worried 'bout Ezra because of the poison."

"Exactly," said Myrtle. "Lucinda is worried about the *appearance* of the poison since Ezra is a botanist. But she wasn't worried that he'd murdered Luther. She said it wasn't in his nature. She was over here because she was concerned that Red was automatically going to think Ezra was responsible because of his job. Sadly, I don't know *what* Red thinks. And now I think we should do something completely different. Chess."

Miles sighed. "I notice you're using the word 'we', but I know you have no plans on actually teaching or playing chess."

"I'm taking a chess sabbatical," said Myrtle with a shrug. "I'd rather be a bystander. Or, perhaps, a cheerleader."

Wanda gave Myrtle a gap-toothed grin. "I could use a cheerleader."

Miles looked as if he wasn't entirely sure how Myrtle could pull off being one. Nevertheless, he obediently pulled out Myrtle's ancient chessboard and the zipper bag of chess pieces and set it up.

Miles seemed to fully expect that it might take Wanda a while to catch on. That might have been because she was listening silently without asking any questions at all. Her eyes were narrowed and focused as she watched him move chess pieces around the board, explaining how each one moved and what each piece's capabilities were.

Miles ended the educational part of the program and said, "Do you have any questions right now?"

Wanda shook her head. "You done good."

"All right." He hesitated. "Would you like to do a sort of practice round?"

"Pooh on practice rounds," said Myrtle. "It's time to get to the nitty-gritty."

Miles made sure all the chess pieces were back where they were supposed to be and let Wanda make the first move. Apparently, she made a good one and Miles raised his eyebrows. Wanda concentrated on the board and seemed to be looking at each piece in turn, thinking about what would happen if she moved it or if Miles did.

Miles carefully made a move and then Wanda countered. Miles raised his eyebrows again and focused very cautiously on his next move.

Miles did win the game. After all, he was about to be part of a chess tournament. There were only a few people he regularly lost to and one of them was Myrtle. But Wanda had done exceedingly well.

"Good job, Wanda!" said Myrtle, fulfilling her role as chess cheerleader.

Wanda gave her gap-toothed grin, looking pleased.

"And you've never played before?" pressed Miles. "Not as a child, even?"

Myrtle said, "For heaven's sake, Miles. From what Wanda has told us about her background, I hardly think chess factored into it."

"First time today," said Wanda.

Miles said, "Then you did very, *very* well Wanda." He looked over at Myrtle. "We should pick her up a chess board at the store."

"Oh, she can take this one home with her. You know I'm done with chess."

Miles looked relieved to hear Myrtle confirm this once again.

Wanda looked thoughtfully at Miles. "Elaine weren't the same, wuz she? Bein' good at chess?"

He shook his head emphatically. "She was not. It's a pity that Elaine doesn't seem to be picking up on the basics of the game as quickly as you just did."

Myrtle added, "Especially since she tries so hard. It makes me a little sad to see her try and try and not have any sort of reward at the end."

Wanda looked very determined. "Be sure she keeps playing."

Myrtle and Miles frowned in confusion. Miles said, "But I don't think that's a very good idea. I'm certainly not going to *discourage* her, but if Elaine comes to the point where she's frustrated and ready to quit, I think that would be the best outcome for everyone."

Wanda shook her head, though, still looking quite resolute. "She needs to keep tryin'. Jest for a while."

Myrtle said, "This all sounds suspiciously like The Sight wending its way into our ordinary lives again. I do wish it operated differently, Wanda. Its vagaries are most disconcerting. That being said, of *course* I'll be sure not to shut Elaine down. She does a ghastly job with all of her pastimes and interests, but I do try to encourage her and her horrid hobbies."

Wanda looked more relaxed at Myrtle's little speech. "Good."

"For all we know, Miles, Wanda could be telling us that Elaine has finally found her perfect pastime. Perhaps she'll go on to become a chess star, become rich and famous, and will support us all."

Miles said dryly, "If that's the case, she must be having a slow start."

Wanda stood up and looked at them apologetically. "Sorry. Think it's time for me to go."

"That's rather abrupt, Wanda. I was planning on feeding you another meal at the very least." Myrtle frowned.

"Dan's about to come. Thanks, though."

Myrtle hurried off to get a cloth tote bag which she filled with the chess board, the pieces, and odds and ends of garden club food that she randomly threw into the bag. Miles topped it off with some of the cash from his wallet.

Wanda gave them a grateful look as suddenly there was a cacophony of sound outside Myrtle's house. "That'll be him," she said simply.

Myrtle and Miles watched as Wanda walked to her brother's truck. Dan, wild-looking as always, gave them a salute before taking back off again as the truck backfired.

Miles said, "I think it's time for me to head back home, too."

Myrtle put her hands on her hips. "You, too? I was going to cook something."

"You gave away most of your food to Wanda."

"Yes, but cooking is a creative endeavor, Miles. I have a little canned chicken, some beans, some cream cheese, some eggs. I'm sure I can come up with something remarkable."

Miles gave a slight shudder. "I'm certain that 'remarkable' is an excellent choice of words. Just the same, I think it's time for me to put my feet up."

"Was it the walk? Or the stadium stairs?"

"Both of them. And the fact that I didn't get enough sleep last night and have had quite a bit of chess today. Chess can be exhausting."

Myrtle said, "Yes, but wasn't Wanda wonderful?"

"She definitely seems to have a propensity for both cards and chess. It's interesting how her brain works. Maybe I'll play chess with her again soon. See you tomorrow, Myrtle."

Chapter Ten

After Miles left, Myrtle did come up with a dinner for herself. She decided not to cook anything fancy but to stick with eggs. She read her book a little bit, but thoughts about the case kept intruding. She finally took out a legal pad and a pen and started jotting down notes about everyone involved with Luther's death and how they connected with each other. There were, she decided, a lot of lines between the different suspects. But then, it was Bradley, North Carolina. Everyone was connected somehow, if not out-and-out related.

A couple of days passed, more quietly than Myrtle liked. Elaine continued her chess game with Miles and it was interrupted once again, this time by some sort of crisis involving Elaine's plumbing. Myrtle believed that they must be acts of God working on Miles's behalf.

Finally, there was something for Myrtle to get out of her house for. Luther Cobb's funeral was that day at noon. Miles was to pick her up and drive Myrtle to the cemetery for the graveside service. In preparation, Myrtle put on her funeral outfit. She ordinarily had always worn a particular dress for funerals but there were such a high number of deaths in Bradley that the garment had become quite worn. It had been replaced by a subdued pant and top which was actually much more preferable since she could more easily wear her sensible shoes with them. When octogenarians were traipsing around cemeteries, it was smart to wear shoes with a certain amount of tread.

The only problem with any of Myrtle's funeral outfit options seemed to be their propensity to attract spills. She couldn't understand it. She'd wear the outfit for three hours, inspect it carefully, see no spots or stains, and hang it up in her closet for the next dearly departed. Then, like magic, she'd pull it out and a stain would be present. She was beginning to think there was some sort of malicious sprite that lived in her closet and soiled her clothing.

Fortunately for that morning's service, the funeral garments were only slightly stained. Myrtle took them into the kitchen and rigorously scrubbed at them until they were perfect. She'd throw them in the washer at the end of Luther's service. She tried not to wash them *every* time because she knew they'd get worn out before their time.

Miles was, as usual, punctual. He wore a dark suit, which never seemed to be spotted with stains. It made Myrtle want to sabotage it during the funeral reception.

"How is everything today?" asked Miles as he drove them over to Grace Hill cemetery, which was about ten minutes away from the center of town.

"Well, it's better because I have something to do," said Myrtle with a shrug.

Miles smiled. "I doubt Luther would appreciate giving you something to relieve your monotony."

"I was even thinking about playing chess with Elaine. *That's* how bad it was."

Miles gave a shiver. Then he decided to change the subject to a lighter topic. "Are you planning on doing any sleuthing during the funeral or reception?"

"Absolutely. I'm counting on Vivian Lawson being there. This should be a prime opportunity for us to speak with her."

Miles raised an eyebrow. "Luther's long-suffering assistant? But he fired her. I have a hard time imagining her wanting to attend his funeral service."

"Maybe she'll simply want to make sure he's dead. Or maybe she'll be there to give emotional support to Luther's wife. After all, Vivian has been involved with the family for a long time. I'm sure Dinah would appreciate having her there."

Miles was craning his head, looking around the cemetery for a likely location. "Do you see any cars?"

Grace Hill had been the premier burial spot in Bradley for the past 150 years. But it was full of old oak trees that blocked views. Myrtle said, "Try around that bend in the road. I know there are some more plots over there."

"I thought that was the old part of the cemetery. Shouldn't those plots all be filled by now?" asked Miles.

Myrtle shrugged again. "Not really. They're family plots . . . oh, you know the type. The family buys a slew of cemetery plots and then there's always room whenever someone kicks the bucket."

"Oh, right. Yes, I have the opportunity to be buried in several different states, I believe. I suppose it just depends on proximity."

They went around the next bend and, sure enough, there were about ten cars collected.

"Seems like a small crowd," said Miles as he carefully piloted the car near the gravesite.

Myrtle scanned the gathering. "I don't know. Considering how awful Luther was, this looks like a pretty good-sized group."

They walked past an ancient group of cement crosses, a couple of old gates marking various family plots, and up to Luther's grave. It was indeed a family plot with different moss-covered tombs proclaiming *Cobb* on them.

The funeral director had set up what looked like a few too many folding chairs. "Let's take a seat near the back," said Myrtle in a quiet voice. "I don't think they're going to need all these chairs and I fancy sitting down for this one."

Miles sat down next to her. "You usually don't mind standing during graveside services."

Myrtle said dryly, "It's the minister."

Miles turned to look at a grim-looking man with thick spectacles and long white robes. "What's wrong with him?"

"He seems to be in love with the sound of his own voice. I've attended quite a few services where he's officiated. It's been fairly miserable. For one service, I didn't have a seat and had to wander away and sit on a grave marker. I'm just not accustomed to standing in one spot for over an hour."

Now Miles looked alarmed. "Over an *hour*?" he hissed.

"We'll be just fine as long as we're seated. Let's see who else is here."

The limousine with Dinah Cobb and the family had yet to arrive. But there were a few notables in the attendees. Red was there, of course. He glowered at her when he spotted her and she gave him a cheery wave.

"I thought Olive Fuller didn't really know Luther," said Miles.

"That's right. Why . . . is she here?"

Miles gave a small nod of his head and sure enough, there was Olive, dressed all in black and holding a tissue.

Myrtle rolled her eyes. "I have the feeling she's here simply because she likes to know things. She wants to be The Informer in her friend group—the one who can fill everyone else in. Let's be sure to try and avoid her at the reception."

Miles said, "I guess Red is here to keep an eye on things."

"You know how Red is. He always thinks that the killer likes to attend their victim's funeral to gloat or something. I'm not sure he's quite correct about that. At any rate, it's sort of entertaining to see him at the services—it makes him so irritated when I'm around asking questions."

"And, for you, it's the questions that make these events worthwhile," said Miles.

"Absolutely. And there's Vivian Lawson, as I suspected. I definitely want to get the chance to speak with her before we leave."

They didn't have a chance to chat more because the soloist started singing to indicate the beginning of the service.

Thirty minutes later, Miles and Myrtle shared a quick look. The minister had launched into a full-fledged sermon by now.

Even Dinah was starting to look restless and it was her own husband's funeral.

After thirty *more* minutes, there was a light at the end of the tunnel as the soloist sang again. However, the minister spoke again after that.

Fifteen more minutes later, the mourners were finally dismissed.

Miles was extremely relieved. "I was going to have to drive away to find a men's room if it went much longer," he murmured.

Myrtle carefully stood up, testing her legs after the long period of disuse. "At least we were sitting down."

"I feel like I've had a couple of weeks' worth of church."

"I can write you an excuse for church, stating that you've gone far beyond your allotted time," said Myrtle.

The limousine was already carting the family off to the reception, which was being held in the church hall. Myrtle and Miles climbed back into the car and followed.

Inside the church hall, the church ladies, clutching large spoons, were standing behind long tables filled with food, ready for the small group to file through.

Myrtle and Miles spoke to Dinah first. She gave Myrtle a hug and shook Miles's hand. "So sweet of you both to come."

They spoke briefly to the rest of the family in the receiving line and then headed off to get food. They piled their plates with comfort food—black-eyed peas, mac-and-cheese, fried okra, fried chicken, buttermilk biscuits, and lemon meringue pie.

Walking away from the food, Miles said under his breath, "There are going to be a ton of leftovers."

"The church ladies will box it all up for Dinah. They probably think that Dinah needs that much food anyway since some of her food was tainted with poison. I bet a crew of them showed up, tossed everything out of Dinah's kitchen, and plan to to replace it with this. Because they know *their* food is safe."

They sat down at a table and Miles took a bite. "Not only is their food safe, it's very, very good."

"Our reward for making it through the service," said Myrtle with a snort.

They ate while glancing around the room. Olive had spotted them and carefully sat at a different table.

"Problems between you and Olive?" asked Miles.

"Oh, she's preposterous. I got annoyed with her at garden club and I suppose she hasn't forgiven me yet. I'll enjoy the break from her presence." Myrtle raised an eyebrow. "Looks like Vivian is looking for a place to sit." She raised her hand and waved Vivian to sit with them.

"And how do you know Vivian?" murmured Miles.

Myrtle shrugged. "By virtue of seeing her around town since she was born. Small town."

Vivian smiled as she reached their table. The smile momentarily brightened her too-serious features. She had the look of someone who was aging quickly despite only being in her thirties. "Hi Miss Myrtle."

Chapter Eleven

"Vivian! So good to see you, my dear. Please have a seat with us."

Vivian did, carefully setting down her plate, full of a hodge-podge of beef casserole, potato salad, barbeque, and corn pudding.

Vivian blushed a little. "It looks like I went a little crazy in the buffet line."

"A perfectly normal reaction to some pretty extraordinary food. You've just arrived at our table too late to see how packed our own plates were," said Myrtle. "By the way, do you know Miles?"

Vivian politely shook his hand. "Good to meet you."

Myrtle said, "I was actually thinking, Vivian, that this service seems to have all the hallmarks of your organizational skills. Did you help Dinah out with the planning?"

Vivian nodded. "She seemed so lost when I visited her. The minister kept leaving messages for her. And leaving more messages. The more messages Dinah got, the more frozen she seemed to become. I finally asked her if she'd like me to get in contact with the church and set it all up." She gave them a wry smile. "But don't blame me for the length of the service."

"Oh, I knew that was a hallmark of this particular pastor. I ensured Miles and I were comfortably seated. And I think it's lovely that you stepped in and helped Dinah out. It all seemed like such a terrible shock to her. It's no wonder that she couldn't think through it. But it was really above and beyond the call of duty for you. I remember that you switched jobs."

That wry smile popped out again. "That's a kind way for you to put it. I was actually fired, as you probably know. There are no secrets in Bradley."

Myrtle nodded. "I did hear that. But I also heard that you'd done absolutely nothing wrong."

"That's very true. But you know what? Now I've got a remote customer service job and I have all this flexibility that I didn't have before. Being a single mom, flexibility means a *lot* to me." Vivian glanced across the room, her gaze resting briefly on Dinah. "Dinah actually helped me find the job. She kept saying she felt guilty about Luther letting me go the way he did. She was the one who gave me a reference and called a friend on my behalf."

Myrtle said, "I'm sure that made Dinah feel better about the whole situation. She's always struck me as a very fair-minded person."

"Exactly. I kept telling her that she shouldn't feel guilty. I mean, I wasn't happy when Luther decided to fire me, but it wasn't like I was going to harbor bad feelings over it. The problem with Luther was that he just didn't have the finesse to smooth things over. I totally accept that he was ready for a change in an assistant. It was just a shock when it happened so quickly."

Myrtle said, "I have to wonder if Dinah often helped clean up after Luther. Socially, I mean."

Vivian nodded. "I'm sure she did. For a while, *I* was the one who played that role. There would sometimes be an occasion where I'd have to write a soothing follow-up email or letter to make a bad situation better. I know Dinah must have done the same. She's been great to try and help me find more work after Luther left me high and dry."

Vivian's tone was very matter-of-fact.

"You're being very practical about all this, I must say, Vivian."

Miles nodded. "I think I wouldn't have felt much like organizing a funeral service for someone who'd recently fired me."

Vivian said, "I didn't really have time to nurse hurt feelings because I had to get food on the table for both me and my child. That didn't leave a lot of minutes for brooding. Besides, I was quickly over it, emotionally. Honestly, it was probably the best thing for my mental health to leave the company. I feel a lot less-stressed now." She glanced at Myrtle. "That's what I was telling Red. Although it *looked* like I had a good motive to do away with Luther, I really didn't."

"Did you have a good alibi for Red, my dear?" asked Myrtle. "That's one way to get him to leave you be."

Vivian snorted. "Unfortunately not. I guess innocent people don't realize they need one. My alibi was a sleeping preschooler, so that didn't do much good. But I sort of got the impression from Red that he believed me. With any luck, he's got better suspects than me."

Miles said, "Since you worked so closely with Luther, do you have any idea who *might* be a better suspect?"

Myrtle gave Miles a somewhat suppressing look. Sidekicks usually needed to be seen and not heard, even if he did broach a good question.

Vivian carefully considered this, frowning. Finally, she said, "I think I'd take a good look at Marshall Sanders."

"At Marshall? Why?" asked Myrtle.

"All I know is that I saw the two of them arguing. I wasn't in earshot, but neither one of them looked very happy, even though Luther did have a sort of smirk on his face. Maybe there's something there."

Then Vivian, apparently tiring of the subject of murder, decided to launch into an entirely different subject. Which is how Miles ended up finding himself in the midst of a discussion about women's scarves and how to wear them.

They all finished up their food and then Vivian said with a smile, "It was good talking to the two of you. I'd better check in with Dinah to see if she needs anything else. Take care."

Myrtle thoughtfully watched Vivian as she walked up to Dinah's table to speak with her.

"Well," said Miles. "That was a very grown-up attitude she had about Luther leaving her in the lurch that way."

"Wasn't it? I can't help but think that perhaps it's a little too pat. Practiced."

Miles frowned. "Really? She seemed very genuine to me."

"She gives the *appearance* of being genuine. But when Luther fired her, it must have been an incredibly stressful and scary time for Vivian. She's the sole provider for a small child. And Vivian knew she hadn't done anything wrong—that she was an excellent assistant. Plus, it's very difficult in a small town to find any sort of quick income replacement."

Miles raised an eyebrow. "You're making the whole situation sound like something out of *Les Misérables*."

"Yes, it's very like a Victor Hugo storyline. Yet she seems so well-adjusted about it; not bitter at all. It's perplexing."

Miles said, "Maybe she just has an 'all's well that ends well' mentality about it."

"I must say you're doing very well with the literary allusions today, Miles."

Myrtle was about to launch into more thoughts on Vivian when a cheery voice behind her said, "Just the lady I was hoping to speak with."

It was Tippy. Myrtle looked suspicious as Tippy carefully folded herself into a seat next to her.

Tippy turned to smile at Miles. "How are you doing, Miles?"

"Pretty well, Tippy, thanks." At funeral services, Miles always considered himself as doing relatively well, considering the alternative.

Tippy beamed at Myrtle. "I was speaking with Red a few minutes ago."

"A highly-ill-advised activity," muttered Myrtle.

"He was telling me that you were looking for things to do. That you'd been feeling a little at a loss lately."

Myrtle's eyes narrowed. She could see where this was heading. "Did he?"

"That's right. It's understandable, isn't it? The heat has been ferocious. Thank goodness it tamped down a little bit for the service today or we'd all have been roasting. I know I've been feeling sort of trapped inside with my air conditioning lately. Anyway, Red mentioned that you might want to help out with chancel guild."

Myrtle gritted her teeth. "That is a fallacy."

Tippy's face fell. "Oh dear. Was it just Red being Red?"

"I'm afraid he's misled you," said Myrtle. "I have no interest in helping out with chancel guild."

Tippy sighed. "Well, it was worth a try, anyway. I guess I should have known Red was just trying to keep you occupied."

The three of them looked across the room where Red was standing near the table of lemonade and iced tea. He had a dour expression on his face, likely because he knew his hopes had been dashed.

Tippy said, "So what are you doing instead, Myrtle? You must have some sort of dangerous pastime that Red is trying to keep you away from."

"It's only dangerous in Red's head. I'm doing a bit of investigative reporting for Sloan. On Luther's death."

Tippy raised a well-groomed eyebrow. "Are you? How is that going? It seemed as though Ezra was the talk of garden club. Do you think he had something to do with Luther's death?"

"I don't. He didn't know Luther and had no motive whatsoever to kill him. I do believe that someone might be setting him up as the fall guy for the murder, though. After all, it seems someone went out of their way to implicate him."

Miles said, "As a matter of fact, Tippy, you'll be doing everyone a favor if you let people know that Ezra had nothing against Luther. He's sort of a friend of Myrtle's and mine."

Tippy knew just about everyone in town. What was more, Tippy was something of a local influencer. If Tippy were to spread word that Ezra wasn't connected with Luther's death at all, that would be the end of it.

"I see," said Tippy slowly. "Yes, of course I'll let everyone know. It's a terrible thing to be wrongfully accused. Good luck with your story for the paper, Myrtle."

"Thanks. Sorry about the chancel guild thing."

Tippy gave her a smile. "Well, you know what they say. If it sounds too good to be true, it probably is."

As Tippy set off for her table, Myrtle said, "Let's make haste before Red tells more old biddies that I want to volunteer."

Miles said as they made a quick exit, "You *do* volunteer, though."

"On my own terms."

They got into the car and Miles drove her home. Myrtle surveyed her funeral outfit. "I don't see a single spot on me."

"You never do. The spots only materialize the next time you have a funeral to attend."

"True. I suppose I'll throw these in the washer when I get home. I'm just trying to preserve the outfit as long as possible. It wasn't cheap," said Myrtle.

"Just make sure to hang it to dry," said Miles with the air of someone who has been taking care of his clothes for a good many years.

Myrtle hopped out of the car when Miles pulled up into the driveway. "Thanks for the ride," she said. "Want to come inside?"

He shook his head. "I would. But I have to play chess with Elaine."

"Mercy. A funeral *and* a charity chess game? You're certainly taking care of your good deeds for the day."

Miles gave her a sad look. "Yes. But maybe Jack will find a way to interrupt this game, too. I can only hope."

Miles's departure meant that Myrtle would spend the rest of the day left to her own devices. She washed and hung up her funeral outfit to dry. She had a crossword puzzle book that Red had given her in the hopes of providing her with a quiet, safe activity. Myrtle quickly finished three puzzles in a row and decided that if anyone wanted to gift her a new puzzle book, it should be full of cryptic crosswords.

Then Pasha came over for a short visit and they watched a bit of a wildlife show, which greatly entertained Myrtle and made Pasha drop off for a long nap on Myrtle's sofa.

When ten o'clock rolled around, Myrtle decided it was time to try and cobble together some sleep. The house somehow still felt very warm so she set the temperature low and got ready for bed.

There she lay awake for twenty minutes. Twenty minutes was the limit for Myrtle in terms of chasing elusive sleep. She got up, unloaded the dishwasher, ironed her now-dry funeral outfit, and did other equally-boring activities before lying in bed again.

At four o'clock, she woke with a start with the strange feeling that she'd overslept. This was quite an unusual sensation for Myrtle. For one, she rarely slept, much less overslept. For another, she didn't have anything in her life that she could possibly oversleep for. There was certainly no reason to set an alarm of any kind.

She got up and proceeded to get ready for her day, that odd feeling of needing to attend to something still looming over her. She dressed, ate breakfast, and flew through several more crosswords while she waited for the newspaper to appear in her driveway.

Then, around five o'clock when she was finally ensconced in her kitchen with coffee and the paper, the phone rang, making her jump. Pasha, who was still hanging around to enjoy the air conditioning, gave Myrtle a reproachful look.

"Hello," answered Myrtle in a breathless voice.

"It's Wanda," croaked a ruined voice on the other end. Identification was unnecessary as soon as Myrtle heard her speak, but Wanda was nothing if not courteous.

"Wanda? Goodness, is something wrong?"

"Not with me. But Ezra is at the park and might need a friendly face," drawled Wanda.

Chapter Twelve

"At the park? Do botanists go to the park at five a.m.? That seems more like a birdwatcher thing to do."

"Don't know," said Wanda, sounding sleepy. "Jest might want to head over there." Having delivered her message, Wanda was now clearly trying to get off the phone and return to her slumbers.

"All right—thanks. Go get some sleep," said Myrtle.

Wanda didn't need to be told twice. She quickly signed off.

Since Myrtle was already completely ready for her day despite the early hour, she walked over to Miles's house. She'd found herself waking Miles up quite a few times lately, so was relieved to see the lights on in his living room. She tapped on the door and Miles, after cautiously looking out the window, opened the door.

"Something wrong?" he asked. "You look as though you're on a mission."

"And usually I'm just on a mission for coffee and company. Wanda called me. She said that Ezra needs our help."

Fortunately, Miles was also ready to leave, despite being somewhat well dressed for the park at five a.m. in khakis and a button-down shirt. They climbed into his Volvo.

"We're heading to Ezra's house?" he asked.

"To the park," said Myrtle.

"This early?" Miles sounded confused. "Who goes to the park at this time of the morning?"

"Botanists," said Myrtle with a shrug.

When they arrived at the park, they saw quite a few police cars and forensics vans. "What kind of trouble exactly was Ezra in?" asked Miles slowly.

"I have no idea. You know how the sight works."

"Or doesn't work," said Miles with a sigh. "It often gives us just a hint of information without really clueing us in on the important stuff."

"At any rate, it certainly sounded as if Wanda had every expectation of us *being* able to help Ezra. She didn't make it sound as if he'd met his Maker." Although Myrtle was getting a sinking feeling in her stomach as she saw the number of emergency vehicles there.

Miles, as usual, was leery about parking near the police cars. Instead, he carefully parked a short distance away, backing into the space so they had a clear view of the park.

"I think we should get out. It's too dark—Ezra won't be able to see us from here." Myrtle got out of the car and Miles, rather unhappily, followed her.

As Myrtle walked up, she surveyed the scene. There was an ambulance there, but the EMTs didn't seem to be in any hurry to help anyone. Then Myrtle stopped. "Isn't that him right there? Ezra?"

Miles peered ahead. "I think so."

"Oh look, he's waving at us! And just like Wanda said, he looks relieved to see a friendly face." Myrtle waved back and soon Ezra, who looked stressed and exhausted, joined them.

"Gracious, what's *happened*, Ezra?" asked Myrtle. "Do you want to come over to my house and talk?"

He shook his head, looking grim. "I don't think I can. Not yet, anyway. I've spoken with Red, but he said the state police wanted to talk to me, too. I'd better stick around."

"What are you doing here so early?" asked Myrtle. "Some sort of botany work?"

Ezra gave a rueful laugh. "No botany, just an attempt at getting some exercise in. I'd *like* to be someone who runs. From time to time, I give running a go since my blood pressure was pretty high at my last physical. Exercise, according to my doctor, is supposed to be a good way to deal with stress."

Miles's expression indicated that he couldn't imagine what could be stressful about botany.

Myrtle, however, said in a knowing way, "Of course it is. So you came to the park to run on the paths before your workday started. But, judging from the various emergency vehicles I'm seeing, you must have made some sort of discovery. Or witnessed a crime of some sort."

Ezra nodded, his face strained. "Yes. Although Red seems to think I *instigated* a crime."

"Well, I'm sure he'll be disabused of that notion soon," said Myrtle.

"I'm not so sure. The problem is that I have no alibi and that I discovered the body."

"Whose body?" asked Myrtle, leaning forward.

"Jasper's. Jasper Hodges." Ezra gave a shiver, despite the fact that it was very warm outside.

Myrtle drew in a breath. "I suppose Jasper was out here exercising, too?"

"He had the right gear on for that." Ezra gave a small shrug, watching the forensics team as they worked nearby.

"And his body?" pressed Myrtle. "Did it look as if Jasper had a natural death? Some sort of coronary event while he was jogging?"

Ezra shook his head and swallowed. "No. There was nothing natural about his death. It looked like someone had hit Jasper over the head with something heavy. Like a crowbar or a tire iron or something."

Myrtle looked grim. "He must have known something."

A voice behind them barked. "Mama!"

Myrtle turned to give her son a sweet smile. "Good morning, Red. Having a busy day so far?"

"What in the blue blazes are you doing here?" He gave Ezra a glare through narrowed eyes that made the botanist shift nervously. "You didn't call her, did you?"

Ezra shook his head vigorously.

"Wanda called me," said Myrtle in a cold voice. "Of course I wanted to come right over at once."

"And you badgered poor Miles to drive you over. So I've got a chain-smoking psychic wandering around my crime scene, too?" Red frowned and glanced around, looking for a thin woman in the faint light.

"Wanda *quit* smoking, Red. For a policeman, you aren't particularly observant. And no, she's not here. That's because she doesn't *have* to be here to know about what's happening. She had a vision of some sort, called me up, and then she went back to sleep."

Red grunted.

Myrtle gestured at Ezra. "I understand you think that poor Ezra might be responsible for Jasper's death."

Red glowered at Ezra for disclosing Jasper's identity to Myrtle. "Mama, you know that I have to follow procedure. Everyone is considered a suspect at first."

"But why on earth would Ezra call you if he'd just killed Jasper?" asked Myrtle. "It simply doesn't make any sense."

Red shrugged and glanced over at Ezra. "Because he's smart. And he could be purposefully doing something a smart person *wouldn't* do, just to make the police look elsewhere."

Ezra said, "Look, I don't even know this guy."

"You knew him well enough to recognize him," said Red.

Myrtle decided that Red's foul mood could be attributed to the early hour. He did seem more irascible than usual.

Ezra sighed. "We live in a small town, which means I can match just about anyone's face with a name. But that doesn't mean that I *know* them. I'm an introverted person and spend a lot of my time by myself. I'm not especially outgoing."

"But people in town seem to know you better than you know them. Some folks have suggested that you're involved in Luther's death."

Ezra stretched his hands out. "Look, people in Bradley can be suspicious of things they don't completely understand. And they don't understand me or what I do. That's why I give these botany talks."

Red said, "I thought you said you did those because you loved talking about plants."

Myrtle glared at him. "For heaven's sake, Red, let the man talk."

Red pressed his lips together.

Ezra said, "I do love talking about plants. But I'm also trying to educate the town about native plants, dangerous plants, and what I do as a botanist. I'm trying to be a little more accepted, in my own way."

Red raised an eyebrow. "And you were here at the park before dawn because of . . . plants? Are you sure you didn't know Jasper would be here for his daily run?"

"I *wasn't* here because of anything to do with botany. I came over because my blood pressure has been high and my doctor recommended I run to help reduce it."

"Then you've probably seen Jasper here at the park sometimes," said Red smoothly. "If you follow a routine. You seem like a routine-oriented kind of guy."

Myrtle frowned at Red's tone.

Ezra shook his head. "I've been too sporadic with my workouts. I haven't been doing them regularly enough to have them become a habit yet. But I have seen Jasper the times that I *have* made it over here."

Red grunted.

Myrtle said in a pointed fashion, "Running *is* good for reducing blood pressure, Red."

"So are mothers that behave themselves," said Red dryly. He turned to Ezra again. "If you didn't have anything to do with Jasper's death, do you have any ideas who might have?"

"I don't. Like I said, I didn't know Jasper, so I don't have any insights as to who might be responsible for this. I'd like to help you out, Red, but I just can't."

Red was about to reply to this when another policeman called out to him. He said, "Okay. You're free to go, Ezra. Just make sure you're available if I need to speak with you again." He headed off to talk to the other officer.

Ezra slumped. "He thinks I'm a double murderer."

"He thinks no such thing," said Myrtle. "He's just not a morning person. It makes him cranky to get up so early."

"I'll have to remember that the next time I find a body," said Ezra dryly. "I have the feeling that I should get out of here as quickly as I can before I'm a suspect in some other crime."

"No exercising?" asked Miles with a smile.

Ezra snorted. "The way my heart has been racing in the last thirty minutes, I've already *had* my workout."

"Before you leave, I did want to ask you a couple of questions. I had the opportunity to speak with Olive," said Myrtle.

Ezra gave a crooked smile. "Sorry about that."

"Yes, it was very trying, as all conversations with Olive are. As you mentioned, Olive does not seem to be a member of your fan club. She seemed positively delighted that you might be involved in all this. Do you think she might be behind it all?"

Ezra considered this idea. "I just have a very hard time reconciling the idea of Olive being a killer."

"Don't underestimate bored old ladies," said Myrtle with a sniff.

Miles hid a smile.

Ezra said, "Then she killed Jasper, too? Out here in the park in the pre-dawn hours?"

Myrtle said, "Let me ask you a question about Jasper. Could you tell if he was already on his run? Or was he warming up or stretching? Because it's one thing chasing an athletic man down a path and killing him with a blunt object and quite another to surprise one who was innocently doing some stretches before jogging."

"Oh, he was definitely just warming up. He was collapsed next to a bench that he'd obviously been using to help him stretch."

Myrtle nodded. "Then anyone of any physical ability could have killed him. I'm assuming there was something Jasper knew that the killer didn't want to have leaked out. And there was something else I wanted to ask you about, too. I understand that Marshall and Lucinda don't have the best of relationships."

Ezra's face darkened a little. "She has to put up with a lot from him. I've told her that she should just leave him, but she's been reluctant to do that. She cares a lot for him."

"Is Marshall jealous about your relationship with Lucinda?"

"Probably. But you know Lucinda and I are just friends."

Myrtle said, "Of course. But that doesn't mean he's not jealous over the fact that you and Lucinda get along better than he and Lucinda do."

Ezra sighed. "I guess so. It seems kind of silly and pointless to me. I'll have to ask Lucinda what her take on it is."

Ezra gave a shiver, despite the heat outside. Miles said, "Myrtle, perhaps we should let Ezra go back home. He looks as if he could use a break."

"Good idea. Ezra, we'll check in with you later on. Maybe pour yourself a strong coffee."

"Perhaps a spiked coffee," suggested Miles helpfully.

Myrtle climbed back into Miles's car as Ezra drove away. "Uh-oh. Red is coming back over," said Myrtle. "Step on it, Miles!"

Miles, never one to step on it, became extremely flustered. In the process of being flustered, he managed to step on the accelerator while the car was still in park. The Volvo's engine revved as if Miles were getting ready to street race. In the side mirror, Myrtle saw Red raise his eyebrows before he tapped on Myrtle's passenger window.

Myrtle gritted her teeth and put the window down.

Red said, "Everything okay, Miles?"

Miles blushed. "Yes. Just a little trouble with the car's order of operations."

Red nodded and then shifted his attention over to his mother. "You're heading back home, right? You're not going to be nosy and end up getting into trouble again?"

Myrtle gave a sniff. "As a matter of fact, I'm *not* going home. Miles and I are going to go to breakfast out."

Red looked concerned at this declaration. "I thought your check wasn't coming in for a while yet."

"I believe I can afford eggs and bacon," said Myrtle coldly.

Red dug in his pocket. "Just in case, here's a little spare cash. Just to make sure to tide you over."

Myrtle took it reluctantly. "Thank you," she said, her teeth gritted again.

"All right. Just be sure to stay out of trouble, like I just said."

Red gave the hood of Miles's car a friendly knock and Miles backed up and slowly took off out of the park.

"I'm always surprised when you take Red up on his offers to pay for things," said Miles. "It doesn't seem to fit in with your personal Declaration of Independence."

"If you knew how many times teenage Red would run to the grocery store for me and never give me my change, you'd understand. It's a matter of remuneration."

"I see. So are we really going to breakfast, or are you just going to pocket the money and use it for other purposes?" asked Miles.

"That depends on how much he gave me this time. Sometimes his spare change is quite a good amount of money. Sometimes it's not. It has to do with when he grocery shops and when Elaine does laundry."

Miles looked so perplexed at this explanation that Myrtle continued, "Red will go to the grocery store and absentmindedly stick the change in his pocket. Elaine has a policy that she gets to keep whatever money hasn't been emptied from Red's pockets when she does the laundry."

"Ah."

Myrtle carefully counted up the money Red had given her. She beamed. "Nearly thirty dollars. So we'll have breakfast and then later on this week I'll drop by the thrift store. If this heat-wave continues, I should invest in another short-sleeved blouse."

It was six o'clock in the morning and the diner's staff was just opening up for the day. The man who unlocked the doors gave them a bob of his head and told them to sit wherever they'd like.

They automatically headed over to the same booth they were sitting at last time. Miles said glumly, "I'm feeling very predictable all of a sudden. We were just here."

Myrtle studied the menu, a frown between her eyebrows.

"I already know what you're going to order," said Miles. "You know there's no need to look at the menu."

"Maybe there are some specials. There could be limited-time-only offers that I'll want to take advantage of."

They both read through the menu carefully. There apparently weren't any such offers.

Myrtle shrugged. "Then I suppose I'll just get my usual for breakfast."

"The lumberjack breakfast," recited Miles.

"How sassy of you, Miles! I'm not that predictable."

"Of course you are. And so am I. Go ahead and tell me what I'm going to order."

Myrtle tilted her head to one side, considering this. "Well, the oatmeal was a disaster last time. I suppose you might be eyeing the spinach and feta egg-white omelet. Another example of your misguided attempts to eat healthy at a diner."

The waitress came over and took their orders. She looked as if she already knew them, too. She didn't even bother to write them down.

The door opened and Myrtle stiffened. "Oh, no. It's Olive Fuller."

Chapter Thirteen

There was nowhere to hide in the diner, which was brightly-lit with florescent lighting. Plus, Myrtle was hardly a short woman, despite her efforts at slouching in the booth.

"I thought you'd *want* to talk with her. She's a suspect, after all," murmured Miles.

"I appear to be allergic to the woman. She makes me sort of itchy." Myrtle rubbed at her forearms.

Olive had spotted them, though. She was nothing if not eagle-eyed. She zoomed in right for their table. "There you are," she said triumphantly, as if she was winning at a game of hide-and-seek. "You're pretty elusive, aren't you, Myrtle? I thought I'd speak with you at the funeral service, but you suddenly disappeared. With Miles."

Olive was clearly going to be starting yet more rumors. This time, the stars of the rumors would be Myrtle and Miles and their completely fictitious romantic relationship.

"Only elusive when elusivity is required," said Myrtle with a shrug. Olive's knowing look annoyed her. She was the type of person who treasured knowing things that others didn't. It made Myrtle want to disclose information to her simply because Myrtle would be the one dispensing information instead of the other way around.

"Miles and I just returned from the scene of another tragic death," she said, folding her hands in her lap and looking solemn.

Olive's eyes opened wide and Myrtle got a stab of satisfaction. "What? Who?"

"Sadly, it was Jasper Hodges. At the park. From blunt force trauma."

Miles hid a smile. It sounded as if Myrtle was playing the game *Clue*.

Olive's eyes, if possible, opened even wider. "You don't say. How *terrible*." But the delighted expression on her face belied her words.

"Where were you before you came over to the diner?" asked Myrtle sweetly.

Olive colored a little. "I was at home. Naturally. I don't wander around town before dawn."

It was a cutting remark aimed directly at Myrtle.

Olive continued, "I was not asleep, though. I was tidying up my house. I try never to be slothful."

Her voice had an annoying self-righteous ring to it that grated on Myrtle's nerves.

Olive added, "However, you and Miles were clearly out before dawn. Did you discover Jasper?" Her voice intimated that perhaps Myrtle and Miles were more involved than just discovering the body—that they might have been responsible for there being a body to begin with.

While Myrtle was rather partial to the idea of an octogenarian master criminal, anything coming out of Olive's mouth was annoying to her at this point. It was almost as if Olive had become Erma Sherman, Myrtle's despised neighbor. She said with a sniff, "We received a phone call from our friend, Wanda, alerting us to the scene of the crime. She's a psychic, as you might know. That's why Miles and I were there." Myrtle set the record straight so that Olive wouldn't start Bonnie and Clyde-type rumors. "How well did you know Jasper?"

Olive shrugged. "I knew him as well as I know everyone in town . . . just a hair. I could recognize him in a line-up. I taught Archie in Sunday school a few years ago. Archie is Jasper's son, if you don't know. I found him a very polite young man who knew a lot about Exodus, if I remember correctly. I can tell that you're asking a lot of really pointed questions, Myrtle. You're looking in the completely wrong direction. I know precisely who's responsible for these crimes."

Myrtle and Miles just stared at her.

Olive preened at having their undivided attention. "Ezra. I happened to notice that his car wasn't in the driveway when I left my house a little while ago."

Myrtle raised her eyebrows. "Wasn't it? If it wasn't there, it's because you were out and about earlier than you said."

Miles cleared his throat. "Ezra had been at the park exercising. However, he was on his way home when Myrtle and I left for the diner."

Olive looked momentarily taken aback. Then she said, "I might have driven around a little bit on my way here. The diner wasn't going to be open unless I dilly-dallied. I drove through some neighborhoods and looked to see whose lights were on. The early-risers. Anyway, everyone with a brain knows it must be Ezra. You say he told you he was exercising?" She snorted when Miles nodded. "That man is hardly a body builder. As much time as he spends outside, you'd think he would be healthier-looking. I'm supposing he was the one who found Jasper. Very convenient, if you ask me."

Myrtle said sharply, "People are doubtful about Ezra because they don't understand him. Their limited intellectual capacity is preventing them from being able to grasp the *concept* of Ezra. He might seem different from most people in town because he's introverted, scholarly, and spends a lot of time with plants and books. That doesn't mean he's a murderer. It's very disappointing to include you in the group of people who don't understand him, Olive."

This clearly stung Olive's pride. "I'll have you know I'm a college graduate." She was quiet for a few moments before saying slowly, "Perhaps I've been a little hasty in judging Ezra, however. I might have gotten defensive when Ezra was being so passionate about my chopping down the old oak tree. He and I do have a lot in common in some ways. I was *also* passionate about the tree—I wanted it down so that I could have a sunny spot in the yard and plant some sun-loving flowers."

The waitress came over with Myrtle and Miles's food. Myrtle dug right in, but Miles looked sadly at the food and waited. He was too much of a gentleman to start eating while someone was speaking with them. Even an unwanted person.

Myrtle said briskly, "It sounds like you should make up with Ezra. Life is too short to have these sorts of disagreements. Plus, it's very handy to be on the good side of a young neighbor. Who knows when you might fall and need help?"

The cogs were already turning in Olive's brain. "Yes, that's true. Although my balance is *excellent*." She threw a scornful look at Myrtle's cane.

Miles interjected before the conversation went downhill, "Thinking back to Jasper, do you know of anyone who might want to harm him?"

Olive shook her head. "No, of course not. My only association with him is through church. Hardly a place where one's animosities are out in the open."

Myrtle was still irritated by Olive in general. She said, "I'm guessing Red will be back over to speak with you again today. About Jasper's death, I mean."

Olive's brow furrowed. "Why on earth would he do that? I haven't even spoken with him a first time."

Myrtle lifted her eyebrows in surprise. "Really? Gracious. But then, I suppose he's been so busy that I really haven't had a chance to speak with Red. And isn't it obvious why he'd want to? You clearly have some enmity toward Ezra. It sure looks as if someone wanted him to take the blame for both Luther's and Jasper's deaths." Myrtle shrugged as if the rest was obvious.

Olive looked completely stunned. It clearly hadn't occurred to her that she could ever be considered a suspect.

"But I didn't even really know Luther or Jasper," she said plaintively.

"That's not the point. The point is making it look as if Ezra killed them," said Myrtle in a cool tone. She glanced across the table and pursed her lips. "Good talking to you, Olive. We shouldn't hold you up from getting breakfast any longer." It was hardly a subtle hint, but then, Myrtle had just basically accused Olive of double homicide.

Olive mumbled a goodbye and slunk away to a table as the diner started filling up with early birds.

"I hope your food isn't cold," said Myrtle with a sniff. "You should have just gone ahead and started eating. Olive isn't worth your gentlemanly codes."

Miles took a large bite of lukewarm spinach and feta cheese omelet. After swallowing it down, he said, "Thanks for dispatching her so rapidly."

Myrtle sighed. "That was mainly because I didn't want to speak with her to begin with. She makes all these passive-aggressive slights towards me." She paused. "Didn't it seem as though she might be about to make up with Ezra, though?"

Miles nodded. "It sounded as if she was realizing they really do have some things in common. And maybe your point about being on good terms with neighbors struck a chord with her."

"Well, I hope she does, only because it will be less-stressful for Ezra to be on good terms with his neighbor. Poor Ezra. He does seem to get himself involved in messes, doesn't he?"

They ate quickly and then left, mainly so Olive wouldn't think of a reason to come over and visit with them again.

When Miles turned onto their street, Myrtle exclaimed, "Look! It's Dusty's truck. And Puddin is at my front door. You see it too, don't you? I'm not just hallucinating? It's not some sort of apparition?"

"I do see them there. It's hard to believe my eyes, though." Miles pulled into Myrtle's driveway.

They got out of the car and Dusty came over to them. "Both feelin' better," he said gruffly. "Gotta get to work."

Myrtle gaped at Puddin, waiting at the front door. "You've brought your own cleaning supplies."

Puddin gave her a scornful look. "'Course I did."

There was no "of course" about it. Myrtle could count on one hand the number of times Puddin had actually brought her own cleaning tools instead of dragging Myrtle's out from under the kitchen sink. But Myrtle was never one to look a gift horse in the mouth. She let Puddin in as Dusty fired up his lawn equipment. Miles waved at Myrtle and left for home—and a nap.

Myrtle watched as Puddin started energetically dusting her tabletops. "What caused this radical change?"

"Hmm?"

"Why are you and Dusty suddenly so motivated to work?" asked Myrtle. "Neither of you could be bothered to even *talk* with me about the possibility of work the other day. I could barely get you to help me with the gnomes."

Puddin paused with her dusting. "Dusty and me want to go to the beach. He's been lookin' it up on the computer. Everything's cheap there right now."

"Because it's the off-season," said Myrtle.

Puddin gave her a suspicious look as she usually did when she didn't totally follow. "Anyway, it's cheap there and it's still hot outside. So we can get in the water an' everything."

"Got it. So you're needing to work hard and make a little money for the trip." Myrtle was still rather stunned at the sight of Puddin cleaning and not watching game shows or trying to get out of work. "What beach are you planning on visiting?"

"Myrtle."

"Pardon?" asked Myrtle.

Puddin looked disdainful again. "The *beach* is Myrtle."

"Oh, of course. Myrtle Beach, on the coast of South Carolina."

"Been there?" asked Puddin as she squirted some lemon cleaner on her dusting rag.

"Not for a very long time. I tend to prefer quiet beaches where no one is there and I can sit under an umbrella for hours and watch the ocean."

Puddin wrinkled up her brow. "What fun is that?"

"It's *relaxing*. It's just a different kind of vacation from the one you're proposing."

Puddin muttered under her breath at this. She ran the dust cloth over the remaining surfaces and then moved into the kitchen. Myrtle followed, mainly because she was so fascinated by seeing a galvanized Puddin.

"Are you planning on keeping up this pace all day?" asked Myrtle as Puddin started wiping down the counters and the cabinet doors.

Puddin shrugged. "More I clean, more money I can make."

"Basic economics," agreed Myrtle. She settled into a kitchen chair and Puddin frowned prodigiously at her.

"You're messing me up being there."

Myrtle said, "Over here? But you're over *there*."

Puddin scowled. "By watchin' me. You're slowin' me down."

So Myrtle moved into the living room again to stay out of the way. She turned on the television and found her last recorded episode of *Tomorrow's Promise*. She fully expected for Puddin to wander out of the kitchen and sit down on the sofa to watch. However, Puddin managed to stay motivated and soon had moved on to the back of the house.

There was a tap on the door and Myrtle walked over to open it. Elaine stood there with Jack, who beamed up at Myrtle.

"Is it okay if I drop by?" asked Elaine. "It looks like you've got all sorts of activity going on here."

"It's like a whirlwind. Puddin and Dusty showed up, eager to work."

Elaine's eyes grew wide. "Really? Did one or both of them have a small stroke?"

"Apparently, they're saving for a trip to Myrtle Beach. Come on in."

Jack went right for the toy box where Myrtle kept the toys for his visits to her house and immediately pulled out two trucks and started making truck noises. Elaine settled on the sofa.

"Can I get you some water? Tea? Or maybe a little food?" asked Myrtle.

Elaine shook her head. "I'm good, thanks. I was just popping by to see how you were doing. I heard that you and Miles had something of an unsettling morning."

"Did we?" asked Myrtle with surprise. "Oh, you mean poor Jasper Hodges at the park. Yes, we were there—Red must have told you."

"Briefly, when he called in to tell me what was going on. He got out of bed really early and abruptly because of a phone call, of course." She chuckled. "Ordinarily, I'd have been wondering what happened and if everything was okay with a pre-dawn phone call. But I was so tired out that I fell right back asleep."

"Keeping up with Jack probably provides lots of good exercise," said Myrtle, looking fondly over at her grandson who was driving the truck up the wall.

"It wasn't even Jack this time. Well, I guess it was to *some* degree, but it was mostly learning to play better chess."

Myrtle said, "Ah. Mental exhaustion. That's pretty much the only kind I get nowadays. It's real, though, isn't it? Did Jack at least let you sleep in a little?"

Elaine nodded. "He was very good this morning. When I finally got up and walked into his room to check on him, he was just sitting quietly on the floor and looking through his books."

"Such a brilliant child," said Myrtle, beaming at him. She looked back at Elaine and said, "Did Red say anything else about Jasper?"

"Not really. Just that you and Miles were there and something to do with Wanda. Was she there, too?"

Myrtle said, "She just called to let us know that something had happened. I rounded up Miles and we headed over to the park." She paused. "I guess Red mentioned that Ezra was there?"

"He did. And I really like Ezra, but it sure doesn't look good for him, does it?" asked Elaine. "Luther is dead from a poisonous plant that Ezra has on his property and then Ezra discovers Jasper's body."

"Things could be better," admitted Myrtle. "But the problem is that Red has a very limited imagination. Things that *look* clear aren't always that straightforward. There are plenty of more-viable candidates as suspects. That's why I need to get to the bottom of this and clear Ezra's name."

Elaine nodded, not seeming in the slightest bit startled to hear her octogenarian mother-in-law stating that she was going to solve two murders.

There was a shriek from the back of the house and a crashing sound and Puddin came flying into the living room.

Chapter Fourteen

Myrtle and Elaine gaped at her. Jack stopped driving his truck momentarily.

Puddin pointed a shaking hand toward the back of the house. "That witch-cat is in there!"

"Pasha is? The poor baby. She must be wondering what that awful screaming was all about." Myrtle marched into her bedroom and carefully picked up Pasha, bringing her back into the living room. "You've scared her to death, Puddin."

"She scared *me* to death! I was mindin' my own bizness and she came outta nowhere!" Puddin said huffily.

"That's completely impossible," said Myrtle. "Nothing can just materialize. It's outside the laws of physics." She stroked Pasha soothingly.

Puddin stomped toward the bedroom again, grumbling all the way. Jack recommenced with his trucks and the requisite truck sounds that accompanied them.

Elaine said wryly, "And I thought things were exciting at *my* house."

Myrtle snorted. "This is Puddin-generated drama. It always seems part of the Puddin package, one way or another."

Elaine said slowly, "She actually seems to be cleaning, though. And Dusty looked to be trimming your bushes outside. I guess the beach trip is very motivating."

"I suppose," said Myrtle with a shrug.

Elaine looked wistful. "A beach trip would be a lot of fun right now."

Myrtle said, "Would it? It's so hot outside and there's never a guarantee of any sort of breeze coming off the water. It sounds like it could be unbearable."

"You're probably right. I guess I'm just looking for an escape of any kind."

Myrtle frowned. "Is everything okay? Is Red driving you up the wall? Because just say the word and I'll speak with him."

Elaine hid a smile. She knew there was nothing Myrtle would like better than an excuse to read Red the riot act. "Red's just fine. I haven't seen that much of him lately, of course."

"So he's *neglecting* you."

"No, no. He's just working, that's all. He's trying to solve the case before the state police do." Elaine paused. "Or before you do, I suppose."

Myrtle preened. "I do seem to have something of a knack for unveiling the perpetrators of these crimes. So, if it's not Red, who is it?"

"It's no one. It's really just me. I need a little bit of a break when I'm not doing things with Jack. You know how I always try to keep my brain stimulated."

Myrtle nodded. Indeed, she did. The problem was Elaine's complete ineptitude at brain stimulation, despite her best ef- forts. Still, Myrtle admired the way she kept trying to find creative ways to fill her time and do something meaningful. When Myrtle was bored, she usually stirred up trouble. Elaine, on the other hand, tried to make something beautiful or learn something. The only problem is that it always went very, very wrong.

"Is chess not working out then?" asked Myrtle delicately. She didn't want to put herself in the position of trying to help Elaine with a hobby. That would set the stage for all sorts of future trouble.

Elaine sighed. "I'm not sure. Miles seems to be trying everything *not* to win our chess games when I'm playing with him. You know what a gentleman he always is."

Myrtle did. He apparently was so much of a gentleman that he didn't want to upset Elaine by winning a chess game in six moves, even if it meant playing a longer game with her.

Elaine continued, "I can see what he's doing, though. I'm starting to come to the conclusion that maybe I'm just not very good at chess."

Myrtle blinked at her. This was the first time that Elaine seemed to have acknowledged defeat. "I'm sure that's not the case," said Myrtle slowly. It was the case, of course, but Elaine seemed so discouraged. "How about if you play a game with someone else?"

"You?" Elaine brightened.

"Oh no . . . you wouldn't want to play a game with me. We've already established that I don't even know the names of all the pieces. What you need to do is play the game on your phone. Set the level to beginner and enjoy the game," said Myrtle.

"I've been playing on the computer, but I haven't been doing too well. Because, you know, it's a computer. Those beat chess masters, don't they?"

"Only if you set the difficulty level too high. The computer is programmed differently for different abilities." At least, this was how Myrtle supposed it all worked.

Elaine smiled. "I bet I don't have the difficulty level set low enough. Maybe I can tweak it and actually win some games and build my confidence. That sounds so much better than making my poor chess partners suffer by trying to let me win. I'm going to give it a go when I get back home. Thanks, Myrtle."

"Happy to help, dear. But it isn't Jack's naptime, is it? How about if you leave him over here to play for a little while and try out the easier computer chess at home so you won't be bothered?"

Elaine thought this was a splendid idea so she hurried off home and Myrtle and Jack played with trucks as Pasha watched them with interest. Puddin hurriedly finished up her cleaning.

Myrtle scrounged up some cash to pay her.

Pudding gave her a shrewd look. "The house could use some spring cleanin.'"

Myrtle narrowed her eyes. "Could it? Or is that just your wallet talking?"

Puddin continued, "There's services that ain't covered by regular cleanin.'"

"Or, as it happens, *sporadic* cleaning."

Puddin frowned. "Wish you'd speak English. Hate it when you start throwin' German words in there."

Myrtle took in a deep breath. "What types of things do you think need to be addressed with this spring cleaning?"

Puddin was delighted to elaborate. "Dustin' light fixtures, wipin' down appliances, vacuumin' curtains, scrubbin' the bathtub. Stuff like that."

Myrtle considered this. "Would it be the new improved Puddin doing this cleaning? Or the usual Puddin?"

Puddin gave her a scornful look. "The Puddin you see right now."

"And how much would this extraordinary service run me?"

Puddin had to think about this for a moment. "Guess it would be an hourly rate."

"Oh no. No, we're not doing an hourly rate because that would reward you for being poky. We'll do a flat fee."

Puddin squished her face up as she carefully thought this through. "Deal."

"No, it's not a deal because you haven't come up with the flat fee yet. I'm an old woman and I'm on social security and a pension. I have to know how much things cost before I pay for them." Plus, Red would try and take over her banking if she mismanaged it. Which she *never did*.

This bartering process could have lasted the rest of the day but fortunately for them both, Dusty stomped through the front door at that point, having finished with the yard work.

Puddin shrieked at him. "Dusty! Shoes!"

Dusty obediently removed the offending shoes so that Puddin didn't have to pull out the vacuum once again. Then Puddin trotted over to confer with Dusty in private about the cost of a special spring cleaning for Myrtle. He immediately came up with an acceptable flat fee amount.

Puddin pulled a small planning calendar out of her purse and poised a pen over it. "When would you like to schedule?" she said in a haughty tone.

Myrtle's mind was so blown by the idea of Puddin actually adhering to a schedule that she had to pause for a moment to collect her thoughts. "Tomorrow? Or the day after?"

Puddin studied her calendar with a focused look on her face. "Reckon I can do tomorrow afternoon. See ya then." And she and Dusty left the house and took off in Dusty's truck.

Myrtle and Jack then helped themselves to a snack in the kitchen. Myrtle kept some special snacks on hand for Jack's visits, which they both looked forward to. They had cheese crackers and graham crackers with peanut butter on them. Then they worked on a puzzle that Myrtle pulled out of the cabinet. It wasn't really a puzzle for small children, but Jack was able to do it . . . further proof in Myrtle's mind of Jack's brilliance.

It was sometime later when the doorbell rang. Elaine was on the front step, looking very happy.

"The chess went well?" Myrtle guessed.

"It did! Well, I still didn't win, but the computer didn't *immediately* beat me, which I thought showed great improvement. I did set it on the novice level, but you have to start somewhere, don't you?"

Myrtle nodded in agreement. And was thinking that Miles would need to think up an excellent reward for her since he wouldn't have to play Elaine anymore.

"How have things been here?" Elaine asked.

"He's been a little angel, as always. And he's helping me with a 100-piece puzzle."

Elaine's eyes grew wide. "Helping you? Are you guiding his hand or something?"

"Not a bit. Like I told you, Jack is a *genius*. He has excellent spatial awareness."

Jack grinned at Elaine and at Myrtle.

"And he's adorable, too," said Myrtle, giving her grandson a hug.

Elaine said, "I'll have to look into getting him some puzzles for home. Maybe they can keep him busy while I practice chess. Thanks, Myrtle."

As Elaine left, Myrtle patted herself on the back for a job well-done. She'd been very helpful today. It made her consider other ways she could be helpful.

It was precisely then that the phone rang.

It was quite a surprise to hear Marshall Sanders on the phone.

"Marshall? How are you?"

Marshall said, "Doing well, thanks, and hope you are. I had a quick question for you. I have a student in one of my classes who's very interested in journalism. She's on the school paper staff and was very interested in maybe helping out at the *Bugle*. But Dakota said that the editor wasn't too keen on the idea of having an intern. And, unfortunately, the staff member who's the advisor for the student newspaper this year isn't all that invested."

Myrtle pressed her lips together tightly at the thought of the *Bugle* not welcoming an intern. She had a feeling that Sloan wasn't keen because he didn't want anyone shadowing him and witnessing his little lunch and late-afternoon visits to the nearby bar. "That's a pity."

Marshall continued, "Since I'd just seen you at the school, you came right to mind. Of course, you were the newspaper advisor, as we'd recently talked about."

"I certainly was. And now, of course, I'm a correspondent at the *Bugle*. And I'd be *happy* to have an intern. I'm pursuing a big story right now, as a matter of fact."

Pasha stopped grooming herself to watch Myrtle with big eyes.

"That sounds perfect," said Marshall. "We'll need to do a quick background check on you and you'll need to fill out some paperwork for the school. The newspaper adviser should be the one doing this, of course, but some things you gotta do yourself to get them done. Dakota is in softball practice right now, but do you think you could run by the school now? By the time I give you the paperwork and get your license, she'll probably be finishing up and you can meet her."

"I'll be over there in just a few minutes."

Which meant that Myrtle called up the long-suffering Miles and cajoled him into driving her over to the high school.

"Are you sure that you want an intern?" asked Miles in a doubtful tone. "It sounds rather intrusive. You spend a good deal of time doing crosswords and watching soap operas and things. Won't you feel pressured to be focused on articles and investigating if you have someone shadowing you?"

"Not a bit. Dakota will be in school most of the time between classes and softball practice. When she's free, she can come by and help me write my article."

Miles said, "You won't be taking her around to speak with suspects?"

"Certainly not! I can't expose a high school student to that type of danger. That would be irresponsible of me. No, my plan is to have her help with the article, perhaps help find photos, and then come up with content for the paper's social media."

Miles looked impressed. "Actually, helping with the paper's social media accounts sounds like a great idea."

"I do some of it for the paper, of course, and Elaine does a few other things. Dakota can really help us have a presence."

"Don't you need to run this by Sloan?" asked Miles slowly.

Myrtle waved a hand airily. "Sloan is always happy to do whatever I ask him."

"I wouldn't say it makes him *happy*," murmured Miles.

"At any rate, what could he possibly have to complain about? Free help? Pfft."

Miles drove carefully into the high school parking lot and into a spot and they walked into the building.

Myrtle took a deep breath. "Ahh. High school. This smell really takes me back."

Miles looked uncomfortable. "It takes me back, too. To a very unhappy time."

"That's because you didn't spend most of your adult years at a high school. For me, I have happy memories. I loved my kids and teaching them. There were a lot of good times."

Miles looked as if he was having trouble reciprocating that sentiment.

Myrtle went to the office and they signed in, getting nametags to wear. The staff called Marshall up to the office and he led them back to his classroom.

"I've got everything set up for you, Miss Myrtle. If you could give me your driver's license. I'm guessing there are not going to be many bad things on your background check." He gave her a teasing smile.

"Nor on my driving record. Considering the fact that I only drive once every couple of months or so." Myrtle sat down in a desk and started filling out the paperwork that Marshall had pulled out for her. "By the way, have you heard the terrible news?"

Marshall looked solemn. "About Jasper Hodges? I'm afraid so. News travels fast around here."

Myrtle said sweetly, "I figured you would have since Ezra would have told Lucinda."

Marshall now looked irritated but was clearly trying to tamp it down. "Yes, I suppose so. I was at home with Lucinda when she got the phone call. I'd just woken up, so I didn't get all the details."

Myrtle said, "I feel horrible for Jasper. He seemed to be such a nice man. And an asset to the community."

"Are people thinking that Jasper was killed as an act of revenge? Like he was the one who murdered Luther and then someone murdered him in return?"

Myrtle thought this was extremely unlikely. For one thing, no one felt passionately enough about Luther to want to exact revenge for his death. But it played into her purposes to let Marshall believe that was a possibility. "Perhaps."

Marshall said slowly, "Well, that's very tough for me to wrap my head around. Jasper was such a great guy." He thought for a moment and then said slowly, "I could maybe see where Jasper killed himself, though. As if he couldn't believe he'd taken a life and decided to take his own in response."

Marshall had apparently not gotten the memo that this was not a suicide. Miles quirked an eyebrow at Myrtle. She said again, "Perhaps."

"It sounds like you knew Jasper well," said Miles.

Marshall nodded. "He was a friend of mine." At this, Marshall started choking up and Myrtle looked on with great concern until he was able to get control of himself again. "He was just an all-around good guy," he continued gruffly. "Good father, good friend. He was helpful at the school—he'd volunteer for stuff here a lot. Maybe he just temporarily lost his mind when he killed Luther."

Myrtle tilted her head to one side questioningly and Marshall continued, "Jasper loved his son more than anything. It really upset him to have Luther threaten to expose Jasper's mistake publicly. He was so proud of Archie. Maybe Jasper was just caught up in the moment and trying to protect his son. Luther wouldn't listen, of course. And Jasper lashed out at him in an out-of-control moment."

Miles cleared his throat. "But it seemed that Jasper was the one who discovered Luther's body . . . alongside Luther's wife."

Marshall shrugged. "Maybe that was just a cover. Jasper wouldn't have wanted to go to jail. Maybe he wanted to come by the house and make it seem like he wanted to talk to Luther when he actually knew he was already dead."

Myrtle found this the most unbelievable explanation of all. If Jasper had been the killer, he wouldn't have known when Luther would eat the poisoned pie—if he would even eat it at all. But she nodded as if it were perfectly sound reasoning.

"But if Jasper *didn't* kill himself?" asked Myrtle.

Marshall said, "Like I said, maybe Luther's family killed Jasper for revenge. Not Dinah, of course—she would never do something like that. But it could have been Luther's brother or uncle or other family. Or maybe there's something we just don't know that has nothing to do with Luther at all. Maybe Ezra, since he was at the park, saw an opportunity to get rid of Jasper."

Myrtle raised her eyebrows. "Why would Ezra do that?"

"Who knows? Like I said, it could be a motive that no one even knows about. Then Ezra reported finding a body to seem innocent to the cops. Just like we were saying with Jasper."

Marshall frowned and added, "You know, there is something I noticed lately. I didn't really think much about it at the time, but Jasper had been acting a little . . . off lately."

"Off?" asked Myrtle.

"Yeah. Like I said, I didn't really think much about it because I figured it must have something to do with his divorce or maybe problems with Archie. But with Jasper being gone, I have to wonder if maybe it was something else."

"Something like what?" Myrtle arched her eyebrows.

"Oh, I don't know." Marshall shifted uncomfortably in his seat. "I'm probably just dreaming the whole thing. But what if Jasper *did* have something to do with Luther's death and has been feeling bad about it? That sort of goes back to supporting the idea that Jasper harmed himself because he felt guilty about killing Luther. Which, like I said, could have been totally accidental."

Myrtle's head was starting to hurt just a tiny bit. "I suppose that's possible." Although it wasn't. Trying to steer the conversation back to less-convoluted territory, Myrtle asked, "How is dear Lucinda handling all this? It's very unsettling having all of these terrible things happening in Bradley, isn't it?"

Marshall sighed. "You've got me, Miss Myrtle. Sometimes it's hard to know exactly what's going on in that head of hers." His face darkened a bit. Then he said, "Well, how about if we go ahead and introduce you to Dakota? I'm sure she's looking forward to any insight you can give her about the journalism business."

"The background check won't have gone through yet, though."

Marshall chuckled. "If your background check doesn't come through clean, I'll be a monkey's uncle, Miss M. As far as I'm concerned, it's just a matter of red tape."

Marshall left the classroom to go locate Dakota. Myrtle said thoughtfully, "That was an excellent demonstration of how rumors spread in Bradley."

Chapter Fifteen

Miles said, "You mean the way that Marshall brought up several different scenarios about Jasper's death?"

"Precisely. He'll have half the town thinking that Jasper killed himself because he was guilty. He'll have the other half thinking that Ezra did it."

"Or a vengeful family member of Luther's," said Miles.

"Of which none likely exist. Luther's brother left town just as soon as he could do so."

They stopped talking as Marshall brought in a thin, eager-looking girl with braces and thick glasses which she absentmindedly shoved up her nose.

Marshall said, "Mrs. Clover, meet Dakota. Dakota, this is Mrs. Clover."

Myrtle put out her hand and Dakota shyly shook it.

Marshall said, "As I mentioned to you, Dakota, Mrs. Clover has a lot of experience both as a teacher who was in charge of the school newspaper, and as a current reporter for the *Bradley Bugle*."

Myrtle beamed at Dakota. "Experience that I'm happy to pass along. I'm currently doing an investigative series for the paper. Would you like to head along to the newspaper office with me? We can meet the editor in person."

Dakota's eyes widened behind the thick glasses. "Sure! If you've got time, I mean."

"Time is one thing I often seem to have an abundance of." Myrtle paused. "You should call your mom, though, and let her know where we're going and make sure it's okay."

Miles hid a smile. Once a teacher, always a teacher. Dakota quickly got her phone out and called her mother. Myrtle asked for the phone at one point and spent the next five minutes regaling her mom on her illustrious days in journalism. Apparently, Dakota's mom was perfectly satisfied with the concept of sending her daughter out on some sort of expedition with the octogenarian reporter and so they set out on their way.

"Mr. Bradford is driving us," explained Myrtle as they headed to the Volvo.

Dakota shoved up her glasses again and asked a bit breathlessly. "You mean you have a chauffeur?"

"It certainly feels that way at times," murmured Miles.

"He's a friend of mine who helps me with my investigating. And still has a car, which is very useful."

Miles drove them over to the newspaper office and parked out front. They hopped out of the car and Myrtle said, "The newspaper isn't the most cheerful of places, I'm afraid. Sloan also doesn't seem to have the capability of organizing things, as you'll see. But it's a very interesting spot. When you go into the archives, there are reams of local history."

Dakota said in a hesitant voice, "I did try to get an internship here. But Mr. Jones said that there weren't any openings."

Myrtle pressed her lips together and then said, "Perhaps we can work something out later. Leave it to me."

Myrtle flung open the door to the newspaper office, causing a bright ray of light (and quite a bit of unseasonable heat and humidity) to enter the dimly-lit newsroom. As her eyes adjusted to the lack of light, she could hear the squeaky wheels of Sloan's wheeled chair as it protested as he whirled around.

"Miss Myrtle," he gasped.

Myrtle led Dakota and Miles into the room. "Hi there, Sloan," she said coolly. "I wanted to introduce you to my new intern."

Sloan blushed all the way to where his receding hairline started. "Ah. Yes." He thrust out a hand to the high school girl. "Pleasure to meet you."

Myrtle quirked a brow. "I understand from the school that the paper couldn't accommodate an intern right now. Such a pity, since it's so vital that young people get access to offices and the chance to experience a line of work so they'll know it will suit them." She glanced over to Sloan's laptop computer screen, which was displaying a computer game. "Apparently, you don't have the time?"

Sloan reddened even more and spread out his hands in appeal. "Honestly, I just don't think I'm suited to having an intern. No disrespect intended, Dakota."

Dakota gave him a smile in return, which Myrtle thought was quite generous under the circumstances.

"Well, my plan is to allow Dakota to shadow me a little as I go about collecting information for my next article."

"The next article?" asked Sloan in a faint voice.

"That's right. The follow-up piece to the article on Luther's demise. This one will focus on Jasper Hodges."

Sloan hurriedly said, "Oh, right. Jasper."

"I thought I might also introduce Dakota to the newspaper's social media presence and have her help with content creation."

Sloan was now looking somewhat more interested than he had previously.

Myrtle finished, "And then, because I do feel she needs exposure to a newsroom, I will help direct Dakota with organizing the newsroom." She looked around her with a miffed expression. "Because it sorely needs it."

Sloan's large forehead wrinkled. "Dakota will be here in the newsroom with me?"

"Not by herself. Because you haven't gone through a background check," said Myrtle, giving him a severe look as if she expected a background check to dredge up all sorts of unsavory information.

Sloan relaxed a bit. "I see. Well, that all sounds like a very good overview." He hesitated. "I suppose I could give Dakota some information about an editor and newspaper publisher's role in the business."

"I suppose you could," said Myrtle, still rather snippily.

Sloan looked vastly relieved when the door to the newsroom opened again and a distraction was provided.

This particular distraction interested Myrtle, too. Dinah Cobb was walking into the newsroom.

Dinah blinked to adjust her eyes to the light and then glanced around her. "Well, hi there, friends," she said brightly.

Luther's widow was clutching a couple of papers and gave them all a smile. Myrtle could tell she looked stressed, however. She wasn't quite the merry widow that others might have expected, since she and Luther apparently had something of a mercurial relationship.

Sloan stood up courteously and said, "I believe you've got some advertising for me?"

"That's right," said Dinah. She gave an almost-apologetic shrug. "I'm trying to stay busy, I think." She looked at Myrtle and Miles. "It's an ad for a charity event that the free clinic is hosting to raise funds."

Sloan's phone rang and he excused himself and walked over to the far end of the newsroom to take it.

Myrtle quickly introduced Dakota and then said to Dinah, "It sounds very sensible to stay busy right now."

Dinah sighed. "It seemed like the best thing to do. I've come to the realization that I'm going to need to sell the house."

"Too big?" asked Miles sympathetically. He and Myrtle had very small houses. Myrtle's was small for financial reasons, but Miles's was small because he disliked the feeling of rattling around in a house that was too big for him.

Dinah gave Miles a smile. Something about the smile made Myrtle wonder if she might be flirting with Miles a little, despite the significant age difference between them. But then, all the widows in Bradley seemed to find Miles irresistible. It was just that Dinah was so recently widowed.

Dinah said, "I think it's too big, yes. But that's not the only reason. It's really bothering me being there with only my memories. And the kitchen used to be my happy place in the house, but now when I'm in there, I can only think about Luther and the terrible way he died. Then there's Jasper's death on top of everything. It makes me feel like this is never going to be wrapped up."

Myrtle was starting to be a bit concerned that Dinah might start crying. She briskly said, "I'm sure the perpetrator will be caught soon. But you're right about poor Jasper. It's a terrible thing." She paused. "I'm guessing Red's been by to speak with you about it all."

Dakota pushed her glasses up her nose and looked on with interest as Myrtle pivoted the conversation into more of an interview.

Dinah, however, didn't seem to realize Myrtle was doing anything other than being sympathetic toward her. "Yes, he has. It's his job, of course, trying to find out what happened to Luther and now to Jasper. But it's sort of unsettling to be on the receiving end of things. I don't suppose Red has shared any information with you, has he? I'm hoping someone else looks like a better suspect than I do right now. I'm sure it's not looking good, though."

"What makes you think that?" asked Myrtle.

"Oh, because the spouse is always the main suspect. At least, that's the way it is on police dramas."

Myrtle said, "Red, sadly, doesn't share a lot of information with me. Were you able to offer him an alibi at all for Jasper's death?"

Dinah shook her head sadly. "Not a bit. I'm in the house alone now, of course, like I was just mentioning. I was trying to sleep and doing a terrible job at it. I'm wishing now that I had just gotten up, dressed, and taken a walk. Then, at least, there might have been some folks commuting to work who would have seen me out. Plus, early morning is really the only good time to do any sort of exercising because it's been so terribly hot." She shrugged helplessly. "Instead, I just tossed and turned and didn't end up getting any extra sleep."

"Have you always had sleep problems?" asked Miles. He blushed a little as if he'd asked something too personal. "It's just that Myrtle and I struggle with sleeping. In our separate homes, of course."

Dinah turned a big smile on him again which confirmed to Myrtle that she was indeed flirting with Miles. It made Myrtle wonder if this was something that was just usual for Dinah and how Luther had felt about that.

"I've always slept really well, actually. I used to just close my eyes and I'd fall asleep within about thirty seconds. Then I was completely unconscious of anything around me for at least eight hours."

Myrtle pressed her lips together, feeling rather annoyed that anyone would have such an experience. Then she said, "That sounds amazing."

Miles said wistfully, "I can't even imagine doing that. I don't think I slept well even when I was a baby."

Myrtle said, "But you're not sleeping like that now, Dinah?"

Dinah shook her head. "It's been a total nightmare. I lie in bed and it's like my mind is just spinning out of control."

Myrtle nodded. She was sadly very accustomed to that phenomenon.

Miles said, "Reading books before you try to sleep can help sometimes."

"It doesn't help me," said Myrtle. "It makes me even more awake than I already was. I'll finish the book, look at the clock, and realize that it's three o'clock in the morning."

Dinah gave her a wry look. "I'll have to jot down what you've been reading. It sounds like your books are a lot more exciting than mine are. Anyway, that's the falling asleep part of it. But then I'm also waking up in the middle of the night."

Myrtle and Miles nodded. "You're preaching to the choir," said Miles.

Dinah sighed. "I just don't ever seem to fall back asleep after I've woken up so late at night. What's more, I'll wake up thirsty or I'll want a small snack but I don't want to head down in the dark to the kitchen. Not after what happened there. So I just stay in my room."

"Have you talked to your doctor about it?" asked Myrtle.

Dinah made a face. "I did. She prescribed me a pill to take, but I don't like taking it. It does help me to sleep, but when I wake up I still feel like I'm dragging—like the pill hasn't really stopped working. I just hate that feeling. So I've been doing all the things I read about that are supposed to help. I don't use a computer before bed. I don't have alcohol in the evenings. I make sure I don't drink anything containing caffeine after two p.m. And I do breathing exercises. So far, nothing has helped."

Myrtle said, "I do feel it's best to get up and do something instead of lying there in bed."

"I like that idea," said Dinah. "I absolutely hate tossing and turning. I can never seem to get comfortable."

"When you get up, though, you must do something *boring*. Nothing stimulating. Don't read thrillers. Do laundry or maybe puzzles."

Miles said dryly, "Perhaps Myrtle isn't the best person to advise one on insomnia."

"Nonsense, Miles! I happen to be an expert on insomnia. I'm just at the stage of my life when I don't *require* as much sleep so I don't fight the insomnia any longer, that's all." Myrtle turned back to Dinah. "With any luck, you'll start to feel less stressed as time goes on."

Dinah nodded. "I hope so. Right now, I'm just trying to get used to living by myself. It's been decades since I have." She said crisply, "I've decided that it's *good* to be alone for a while. I'm not in a hurry to start seeing anyone, that's for sure. I'm starting to think I don't do a wonderful job picking men to be in relationships with." She flushed. "I hope you both don't think I'm out of line talking like this. But you both are so sensible and my mind has just been spinning with everything in it. Luther and I didn't have the happiest of marriages. I can't blame him for all of it, though—I was half of the partnership. Anyway, I've been reading Wanda's columns lately. You know how she personalizes them?"

They nodded.

"Well, she did one for me yesterday."

"In the paper?" Myrtle frowned. She'd read the newspaper from end to end and hadn't seen a single mention of Dinah in there.

Dinah shook her head. "Don't think I've lost my mind entirely, but I drove out to her house."

"That must have been an adventure," said Miles dryly.

"It's a unique place to live," answered Dinah diplomatically. "And her brother is . . . interesting."

"Oh, you got to see Crazy Dan, too. And you *still* didn't sleep last night? I find the experience of dealing with Dan to be completely exhausting," said Myrtle.

"I might have slept a touch better last night. Anyway, when I met with Wanda, she explained that the universe was sending me a sign. She initially hesitated when I asked her to give me relationship advice."

Miles smiled. "She would likely consider that out of her wheelhouse."

Wanda, as far as Myrtle and Miles knew, had never been married.

Myrtle asked, "What advice did Wanda give you?"

"She told me that I needed to recalibrate," said Dinah.

Myrtle quirked an eyebrow. "Wanda said *that*?"

Dinah grinned at her. "Well, no, not exactly. But that was the gist of what she was saying to me. She advised me to steer clear of dating for a year or more and just get accustomed to being by myself again for a while."

"Sound advice," noted Myrtle.

"I thought so. Especially since being on my own has been harder than I thought it would be. It's been such a long time since I was single. I really do need to sell the house. The only problem is that Luther and I had so much *stuff*. The idea of going through everything and deciding what to keep, give away, and toss seems like this insurmountable task."

Myrtle thought with satisfaction of her own sparsely-furnished small home.

Miles said, "I think there are services that can help with that sort of thing. I've seen them advertised in the paper. They help declutter and organize and so forth."

"I've thought about using them, too. Right now, though, I think I've decided to stay put for the time being. Get ahold of myself first and proceed from there," said Dinah.

Myrtle said, "That's probably wise. You're still dealing with a lot of stress right now. Perhaps Red will wrap things up soon and that will provide some closure for you. Have you given more thought to who might be responsible for all this?"

Dakota seemed to lean in a little to listen a bit better.

Dinah said ruefully, "That's probably the main reason I haven't been sleeping well. I keep mulling over in my head who might have disliked Luther enough to send him a poisoned pie." She sighed. "My mind somehow keeps coming back to Vivian. And I just hate that because I really like her and think my husband was very unkind and unfair to her."

"I hear you've been very generous to Vivian," said Myrtle.

Dinah blushed a little at the fact that she was now throwing her under the bus. "I've tried. Like I said, I've felt bad about the way Luther treated her. He fired her and Vivian was suddenly out of work and needing to care for her small child. But recently, I was talking to someone who came to the house to express their condolences—someone from Luther's office. He warned me that Vivian had been really furious with Luther for the way he'd treated her . . . that there had been a big scene when Luther fired her."

"Vivian didn't go quietly then," said Myrtle thoughtfully.

"Exactly. Luther's coworker said that he wouldn't be surprised if Vivian had been angry at both Luther *and* me, by extension." Dinah gave a little shake as if to rid herself of the unwelcome thought.

Dakota's eyes were wide behind the thick glasses and she looked rapt as if watching a drama play out on television. "But you were helping her!"

Dinah gave the teen a surprised look as if she'd forgotten she was there. "Yes, but sometimes you really can't make up for another person's wrong."

"At least you helped find her a job," said Miles. "That would have been the biggest cause of concern at that point."

"That's true," said Dinah. "I was really worried about her. She seemed so alone in the world—just Vivian and her son. A single mom who suddenly didn't have a source of income."

Myrtle asked, "Can you picture Vivian doing something like this?"

Dinah shook her head slowly. "Not really. That is, I'm kind of haunted by the thought that she *could*. I know she was angry. But I know the police think poisoning is sort of a woman's crime—a more passive way to kill someone. And it was rather methodical—someone had to research the berries online, procure them, buy a pie, insert the berries in the pie, and then deliver it. Vivian is nothing if not methodical. I just can't picture her doing something so awful, though."

Myrtle asked, "How many people do you think know that you're not a dessert person? Do you think it's reasonable that the perpetrator felt confident that you wouldn't be harmed by the pie?"

Dinah sighed. "Probably not very many people. Whenever I've gone to people's houses for lunch or dinner, it's always easy to just say their meal was so delicious and that I'm stuffed. That way I don't have to explain that I just don't have much of a sweet tooth. Everybody else seems to have one. The times I've told people I don't like desserts, they stare at me like I'm an alien or something." She glanced over at the clock and said, "I really should get going. Good to meet you, Dakota."

Chapter Sixteen

After she walked out, Dakota said in her small voice, "You're great at this, Miss Myrtle."

Myrtle straightened a little. "I am, aren't I? It's the nice thing about being an octogenarian—you get to fly under the radar. People will open up and say all sorts of things to me and never hold my nosiness against me."

"Are you going to write a story about Mrs. Cobb?" asked Dakota.

"Oh no. No, that was completely off-the-record. What it *is* good for is background information and for asking other people questions, too."

Sloan finally wrapped up his phone call and came reluctantly back to join them.

Myrtle said, "Let's give Dakota a story, Sloan."

Sloan looked rather alarmed. "I was thinking we were just talking about shadowing and some social media work, Miss Myrtle."

"We were, but Dakota seems very bright and interested. We should give her an opportunity."

Sloan shifted uneasily on his feet. "The only problem with that, Miss Myrtle, is that I'm already pretty slammed with work. Editing can be . . . well, it can be time-consuming." He gave Dakota an apologetic look for doubting her grammatical abilities.

"*I* will do any necessary editing myself."

Dakota looked a bit uncertain. "That's really nice of you, Miss Myrtle, but I don't know about me handling a story yet."

"Nonsense. You write for the high school paper, don't you? There's not a lot of difference, aside from the fact that the *Bugle* covers more things like award-winning recipes and honor roll lists."

Miles hid a smile as Sloan's face fell at this assessment.

Sloan said slowly, "We do have a family reunion that needs covering. It's actually taking place starting today and going into tomorrow. I was going to run over there myself in a few minutes, take a few pictures, and write up a little something. It would be great if it could run in the paper a couple of days from now."

Dakota lit up. "Really? That would be great."

"See how earnest and enthusiastic Dakota is, Sloan? No one else would call that type of assignment 'great.'"

Sloan nodded and pulled out one of the many loose bits of paper on his desk. "Here's the address. They're at the park at a picnic shelter. It's the Tolly family."

Myrtle said, "The Tolly family is at least interesting. They're sure to have lots of food there, too. And they'll want to ply you with it, Dakota. They like feeding people, whether they know them well or not."

Dakota carefully studied the piece of paper. "Got it. Thanks so much, Mr. Jones."

Myrtle said, "Would you like me to go with you and introduce you around?"

Dakota shook her head. "Mr. Sanders said to make sure I didn't take up too much of your time. I'll have my mom drive me out there and back. Thanks, though."

"Just email the story to me when you're done, dear. And tomorrow, maybe we can work on getting some material for the paper's social media papers," said Myrtle.

The idea of Dakota working on social media made Sloan look much happier. He quickly made up a press badge for Dakota to wear while representing the paper.

Having accomplished her mission, Myrtle was ready to leave. She and Miles told Sloan and Dakota goodbye and headed out the door and nearly straight into Lucinda.

Lucinda gave them a smile. "Well, it's good to see you both. I was running a boring errand and just happened into you."

"Almost literally," said Miles dryly. "The *Bugle* office is so dim that we were blinded by the sunlight outside."

Myrtle said, "I just saw your husband a little while ago. He got me set up with an intern for my work at the newspaper."

Lucinda raised her eyebrows. "Really? I didn't realize he was helping out with the student newspaper at the high school."

"He's not, but he said that the current adviser isn't really invested in her role. Dakota is a student in one of Marshall's classes. Anyway, it was nice of him."

Lucinda looked pleased. "I'm not surprised he'd do something like that. He's always trying to find ways to help out his students. He's a great teacher, of course, but he's a real mentor, too."

Myrtle decided to change subjects. "We also talked a little about what happened with Jasper. Wasn't that a terrible thing? And poor Ezra for getting involved in it again."

Lucinda quickly said, "Oh, but Ezra had nothing to do with it. He was horrified when he found Jasper. I felt so terrible for him. I checked on him a little while ago and he's just exhausted from all this."

"I can imagine," said Myrtle.

"It was just one of those strange coincidences," said Lucinda. "Besides, everyone knows that Jasper ran at the park before he'd head off to work. He's one of those guys who really followed a fitness routine. Surely Red is looking at other people besides Ezra." She gave Myrtle a worried, piercing look."

Myrtle sighed. "As I told you earlier, I don't have any idea what goes on with Red's investigations. But I'm sure he must have other people he's talking to."

Lucinda's brow creased. "I hope so. Well, I'd better head off to the store. Good seeing you two."

They climbed into Miles's car and he drove back to Myrtle's house. He said, "It was nice of you to advocate for Dakota that way."

"Well, it was annoying that Sloan wasn't being very helpful. I felt I needed to step in and help her out."

"It sounded like he's very busy right now," said Miles diplomatically.

Myrtle snorted. "Busy drinking beer, maybe. He clearly just didn't want to take the time to help a young person discover more about an occupation she's interested in. Good thing there are people like me around."

"I wonder what her story is going to look like," said Miles slowly as he pulled the car into Myrtle's driveway.

Myrtle sighed. "I'm afraid it might have all sorts of errors in it. But it couldn't be as bad as Wanda's horoscopes and I manage to decipher those every week. I keep reading things online about texting doing a lot of damage to the younger generation's writing ability. But to me, that doesn't make much sense. After all, texting means that they're writing *more*. I think they're writing a ton more than we used to at that age, Miles."

Miles thought about this. "We wrote letters, though. Lots of letters."

"Yes, but we didn't write letters every *day*. We mostly wrote letters to absent grandparents or when we were deposited at camp or to send a thank you for a gift."

"True." Miles looked surprised at the idea that perhaps the teens of today might actually have more practice writing than he did.

"I will say, though, that their penmanship is practically non-existent," said Myrtle with a sniff. "Too much typing and not enough longhand." She paused. "Would you like to come in?"

Miles shook his head. "I think I'd like to cook myself some supper and just relax for a while. It's been a rather active day."

"Has it? Well, if you're worn out, you should definitely head home. I'm going to come up with some directions for Dakota on the social media updates for the paper—sort of a dos and don'ts type of thing."

After Miles drove away, Myrtle let herself in and surveyed her unusually-sparkling home. It was a testament to what Puddin could actually accomplish if she put her mind to it. She decided she'd do well to eat, too, and heated up some canned tomato soup and made herself a grilled cheese sandwich. The smells of cooking prompted Pasha to look into her cracked kitchen window.

"There you are! Sorry, but I can't leave the window open too high in this heat or my cooling bill would be crazy."

Pasha accepted this apology and Myrtle opened the window more to let the black cat in. She opened a can of cat food and scooped half of it into a bowl, knowing that Pasha was already getting much of her nutrition from decimating the population of small rodents that unwisely lived in the neighborhood.

After eating, Myrtle and Pasha went into the living room to watch a little television. Myrtle had decided that Pasha was a fan of nature documentaries, so she found one on the public television station. The program had lots of meerkats bobbing up and down and Pasha watched the TV with interest, occasionally swishing her tail.

Before Myrtle turned in, she checked her email and was surprised to see a message from Dakota with an attachment. Sure enough, the student had already finished her story.

Myrtle opened it, not having much hope that anything interesting could be made from the Tolly family reunion. She skimmed the piece and raised her eyebrows. Dakota had deftly changed the focus of the story from a mere piece about a cookout and family gathering to a profile of the patriarch, his war memories, the importance of family to him, and his hopes for the future for the Tolly clan. It was a well-written, amazingly eloquent piece. What was more, there was only one small, rather fussy, bit that needed to be corrected. Myrtle inserted a semicolon and that was the extent of her editing. She emailed the article over to Sloan.

Then she looked at her calendar. As expected, it had nothing on it, which had been the source of her recent grumblings to Miles. She noticed it would be Sunday in two days and decided she'd go to church. This was not the norm for Myrtle, but she recalled that Vivian Lawson was quite the church-goer. It might present a good opportunity for her to speak with her again.

Myrtle picked up the phone and dialed Miles.

"Hello?" asked Miles, sounding very groggy.

"Are you asleep?"

Miles said, "I believe that should be in the past tense."

"Hm. You must really have been tired out from our day."

Miles said, "I believe my sleeping had more to do with the fact that it's after midnight."

"Oh. So it is. I was just calling to see if you'd like to attend church with me Sunday"

Miles sighed. "You sound rather fervent about it."

Myrtle said with a sniff. "Religion demands at least a smidgeon of fervency, Miles."

Miles considered this somewhat startling statement from Myrtle. "It all seems very sudden. And I'm a different denomination than you are. We don't ordinarily attend church together."

"You make it sound like we have deep religious differences. When, in truth, I'm Methodist and you're Presbyterian."

Miles said, "Yes. But it all gets somewhat confusing when the Apostles' Creed and the Lord's Prayer occurs. I'll mention the Holy Ghost and you'll be stridently talking about the Holy Spirit. Then there's the whole matter about trespassing."

Myrtle snorted. "It's not as if we're talking about sneaking into Farmer Brown's apple orchard. It's *trespasses*."

"I prefer the *debts and debtors* wording. And I can't help but think you have an ulterior motive for all this."

She sighed. "Okay, I'll admit that I'm hoping we can see Vivian Lawson there. I recall that she attends religiously. No pun intended."

Miles yawned. "Fine. I'll agree to anything as long as I can get off the phone and go back to sleep."

Myrtle hung up the phone with satisfaction. Walking to church was possible but definitely a bit of a stretch, particularly in this heat. If she'd called Elaine and Red and asked for a ride, it would have opened her up to a bunch of questions about her intentions.

Her plan for Sunday set, Myrtle managed to get into bed and actually fall into a marvelous, dreamless sleep for hours.

She spent a very quiet Saturday at home. Considering how busy everything had been lately, it was surprisingly pleasant to be quiet. When she woke up Sunday morning, she made herself a good breakfast and worked her crossword puzzle. Then she set about looking for something appropriate to wear to church. Although she'd finally decided that slacks were fine for funerals, she hadn't quite managed to ascribe to that point of view for church. She also still strongly felt that dresses should be worn with pantyhose or tights of some kind. Rummaging through a drawer, she realized that her collection of nylons was not in the best shape. She managed to find a pair without too many picks and pills. Her church dress, a rather dour-looking black number with a grim bow at the neckline, looked exhausted. Myrtle wasn't quite sure why the dress was so fatigued considering the fact that it had such irregular usage. With limited choices, Myrtle made do with what she had available.

Miles came promptly at eight o'clock. "I figured you'd want to go to the early service and not the eleven o'clock."

Myrtle frowned. "I have no idea which service Vivian might like attending."

Miles, dressed very nicely in a suit and tie, frowned too. "I don't want to go to *two* church services. That might be seen in town as rather odd. It's one thing if you're a member of the choir—they *have* to go to both. People might talk."

"Talk? About two elderly people attending church? There's not a lot of material for them to gossip over."

"Isn't there?" asked Miles. "Won't they assume we're trying to make reparations for some sort of horrid sin?"

"Ah. Well, there's that. In Bradley, the townspeople are gifted with rather active imaginations. Let's just go. I'm thinking that a young woman with a young child would most likely want to attend the early service. Young children wake up early and they sometimes need late-morning naps."

"Do they?" Miles looked uncertain. "How old is this child we're talking about? You're making it sound like an infant."

Myrtle shrugged. "Who knows? It's definitely not a teenager, though. Let's just go. Otherwise, we might not be able to find a good place to sit."

Myrtle's idea of a good place to sit ended up being the balcony. The idea behind it was that she could see everyone from up there, at least when they stood to sing hymns. Which did, actually, seem to be a lot of the time.

"Lots of hymns," Miles observed gruffly. They were the only people who had ventured into the balcony, so it was safe to talk.

"Indeed. Although it's fun looking at the dates on them. They're really pulling out some oldies but goodies."

Miles said, "They're not exactly a collection of top-40 hits from fifty years ago."

"No." Myrtle peered at the small print of the current hymn. "Isaac Watts was the composer in 1719. 'O God, Our Help in Ages Past.'" She glanced around the sanctuary again. "Look! It's Vivian."

"She's pretty late."

"Well, she would have had to drop off her infant/child in the nursery. Whichever it is. That takes time and sometimes they cry. It makes it all very complicated," said Myrtle as if she was someone who knew.

There were more hymns, an offering (Miles chipped in since Myrtle's church purse had no money in it), the Lord's Prayer (Miles managed with the spirits and the trespasses), and then the sermon. It was actually a very good sermon and Myrtle and Miles were quite attentive during it.

Miles murmured, "He's got a rather lyrical way with words."

"Perhaps we should become more regular attendees," agreed Myrtle.

Miles wasn't willing to go that far. "I wonder if they post their sermons online."

"Everything is online. The whole service. You can either just listen to it or you can watch it," said Myrtle. She raised her brows. "You might be converted to Methodism, then?"

"I just want to listen to the sermons," said Miles stiffly.

Then, abruptly, the service drew to a close. Myrtle grabbed Miles. "Let's arrange to bump casually into Vivian before she has to pick her child up at the nursery."

Myrtle managed to hurry downstairs from the balcony, waving away the help a church usher was trying to offer her.

When they reached the bottom of the staircase, there was another obstacle. It was Tippy, looking very surprised to see them there.

"Myrtle! Miles!" Tippy, dressed in a beautiful orange dress that no one else would have been able to pull off, stared at them.

"Hi Tippy." Myrtle bared her teeth in a smile. "We're in rather a rush right now."

Tippy didn't seem to absorb that point, being in shock at seeing Myrtle at church. "I'm just so glad to see you both here. What a treat. Miles, are you considering joining our church? I'm on the new member committee."

Of course she was. Myrtle looked down the church aisle to see what Vivian was doing. Fortunately, she was chatting with another church member.

Miles was shifting uncomfortably at Tippy's question. "I'm just here to support Myrtle," he said, shooting Myrtle a dark look. He added politely, "The sermon was excellent, though."

Tippy turned her attentions on Myrtle. "If you're able to attend church again, I can add you to the list."

"List?" asked Myrtle vaguely as she watched the conversation Vivian was in end.

"Yes. I'm on a committee for that, too. We have a church bus that travels around and picks up our seniors to bring them to church. Our drivers are *excellent*, certified, and all-volunteer."

Myrtle did not want to ride on a bus full of seniors to church each Sunday. And, with Vivian making a swift escape, she really needed to end her conversation with Tippy. "I'm sorry to have to cut this short, Tippy, but Miles and I were rushing out because we needed to find a restroom."

Miles looked very unhappy at the excuse Myrtle had devised. He shot her another dark look.

Tippy, who always maintained the delicacies, flushed a little. "Oh goodness. Of course. I'll just check in with you again, Myrtle. On the bus."

Myrtle gave her a tight smile and moved into the sanctuary with Miles following as Tippy walked over to speak with the minister.

Chapter Seventeen

"Vivian is going the opposite direction," Miles observed astutely.

"Heading right for the children's wing. I know a shortcut. We just have to approach the wing from the outside."

Unfortunately, it was still very hot and humid outside. Myrtle and Miles, due to their advanced age, no longer perspired much. But the humidity did a number on their hair. Myrtle's cane thumped dramatically on the sidewalk as she rushed for the children's wing.

"I'm not sure what excuse we can give for being in this particular area," said Miles.

"Vivian will be so busy with her child, she won't think a thing of it," said Myrtle with a shrug.

But Vivian did blink with surprise at the spectacle of Myrtle and Miles bursting through a side door into the children's wing. They gasped for breath from the sudden exercise and the flight of stairs they'd scaled.

"Are you both all right?" asked Vivian with concern. "Here, let's head to the parlor where you can sit down."

That suited Myrtle's purposes just fine. She melodramatically hobbled next to Vivian, who took her arm and led her to a silk sofa in the church parlor. Miles, red in the face from the exertion or from having Vivian treat them like invalids, sat down in a silk armchair.

"I'll find you some water," said Vivian, immediately taking charge. She strode out of the parlor and farther into the children's wing.

"You can see where she would be an excellent assistant," mused Myrtle, her breath starting to steady again. "She seems very organized and take-charge."

"And she's nice to seniors," added Miles. He still looked rather dejected at having Vivian think they were having concurrent heart attacks.

Vivian hurried back into the parlor with two paper cups filled with water. "Do you need some aspirin?" she asked solicitously.

Miles gave a small sigh. Vivian had indeed suspected heart attacks for them.

Myrtle, still playing to her audience, shook her head and gave Vivian a weak smile. She put a fluttery hand to her throat. "We were just overcome for a few minutes, I'm afraid. I'm so sorry we're keeping you here."

Vivian slowly sat down, realizing that Myrtle wanted her to stay for a while instead of dashing off to pick up her child in the nursery. "That's completely fine. I'll just make sure you both are feeling well again before I head back off."

Myrtle shone that weak smile at her again. "I'm sure it probably has something to do with the ghastly past week we've all had. All the awful news. It takes a toll on a body, don't you think?"

Vivian nodded. "Poor Jasper. I was shocked when I heard the news. That must have been so frightening for him—at the park, alone, in the dark. Then someone comes at you out of the darkness." She gave a shiver and then gave them an apologetic look. "I'm sorry. You're trying to recover from the stress of the week and a health episode and here I am making things worse."

Myrtle quickly said, "Not at all. I think it would be better if we talked it over. Don't you think so, Miles?"

Miles dutifully agreed.

Vivian said, "All right then." She hesitated then added, "Red came to see me again after Jasper's death. Do you know if that's something he did for everyone he spoke to after Luther died?"

"As far as I know. He has a particular protocol he has to follow." Myrtle waved her hands in the air to indicate the ephemeral nature of the protocol.

"I see. Well, I'm afraid I didn't help myself all that much." Vivian gave a grim smile. "I was at home with my little one and he's not much of an alibi. I'm sure I was awake when it happened, though, because Zack is relentless about waking me up before dawn."

"How awful," murmured Myrtle.

Miles quirked an eyebrow at her. Myrtle was ordinarily up far before dawn.

Vivian said, "Oh, it's not so bad now that I'm used to it. We have a little routine now. I get his breakfast together—Cheerio cereal—and his sippy cup. Then I make coffee. The coffee doesn't kick in right away, though, so I turn on the television and he watches cartoons while I doze on the sofa. That's the gist of my meager alibi. I certainly didn't leave the house."

"That early wake-up time must be tough for working a job," noted Miles solicitously.

"Actually, it's much better now because with my new job I'm working totally remote. It's so much more flexible than working for Luther was. It's made me reflect that everything happens for a reason. If Luther hadn't fired me and Dinah hadn't helped me find this job, my life would be a lot more complicated right now. Before, I'd get up before dawn with Zack, get him ready for daycare, pack up a bag and a lunch for him, pack a lunch for me, drop off Zack, then head to the office. Luther always had me work a very full day, too," added Vivian ruefully.

Myrtle asked, "How do you manage Zack at home while you're working?"

"Well, part of the time he's at preschool here at the church. He's enrolled four days a week. Then, at home, he's good to stay on a schedule. He takes very reliable naps in the afternoon after preschool is over."

Miles said wryly, "That might have something to do with his early mornings."

"Exactly! But now I'm getting so much work done while he's asleep that I don't want to get rid of the naptimes. Anyway, I have so much more time with Zack than I did when I worked for Luther. Plus, I'm not as frantic in the mornings anymore. The church preschool doesn't start until 9:00. The biggest thing is that I'm not as irritable and anxious anymore. I'm a lot more relaxed and Zack and I have a closer bond. When I worked for Luther, I felt guilty all the time. I either felt like I wasn't doing a good job for Luther because I'd be worried about the sniffles Zack had when I sent him off to daycare or I'd feel guilty because I sent Zack to daycare feeling under-the-weather."

Myrtle gave her a sympathetic look. "You were caught between a rock and a hard place."

Vivian said, "You sound like you know what that feels like."

"Oh, I do, my dear. I was a single mom myself. My husband died when Red was a young boy and I had to go back to teaching. It was quite a time." Myrtle paused. "So you actually feel like you came out better after Luther fired you."

"I do. I know I did say some really awful things about Luther after I was fired; I didn't react well to him getting rid of me like that. I feel terrible about the way I acted. I was just feeling desperate and worried and lashed out. That's not who I am as a person. But I would never have hurt Luther. I hope Red knows that. And I barely know Jasper, although I feel awful about what's happened to him. I would never endanger my child by putting myself in the position of being arrested. Zack would be alone in the world then."

"Do you have any more thoughts about who might have done this?" asked Myrtle. "You did know Luther so well."

Vivian sighed. "I've been thinking it over a lot. He did have the ability to really rile people up. But I keep coming back to the fact that Dinah really had the most to gain from Luther's death." She flushed. "I sound so ungrateful saying that. She's helped me so much with getting back on my feet."

Myrtle said, "Well, they say the spouse is always the primary suspect."

Vivian nodded. "She could easily have picked up the pie herself and doctored it at the house and just said that it was one of the foods that others brought over. It was a good time to use poison because so many people were bringing by casseroles and desserts."

Miles cleared his throat. "And you'd said they didn't have the happiest marriage. From what you could see."

"Right. Of course, we don't ever really know what's going on in someone's personal life, do we? But from what I could tell from my involvement with Luther and Dinah, they did seem to be oddly-matched. They argued quite a bit—I don't believe they even thought twice about it. Their arguing was practically a habit."

Myrtle said, "I suppose Luther was fairly well-off financially? As far as you know?"

Vivian nodded again. "He certainly was never a big spender. It wasn't as if he hoarded his money, but he didn't spend a lot of it. The business was always doing well, too. I'm sure Dinah is in an excellent financial position now." She shrugged. "Again, I really hate saying this stuff. Dinah has been amazing to me. But I can't figure out who might have benefitted more from Luther's death."

Vivian took a quick glance at her watch and then said apologetically, "If you're both feeling better, I should probably pick my son up now."

Myrtle was about to thank Vivian and send her on her way when someone who'd been swiftly walking past the door to the parlor suddenly stopped and poked her head in. Myrtle sighed. It was Tippy.

Tippy smiled at them. "Are you three having a party in here?"

Vivian stood up, looking relieved. "No. Myrtle and Miles had a bit of an . . . episode. They weren't feeling well. Actually, Tippy, if you could sit with them until they're fully recovered? I have to pick up my son from the church nursery."

Tippy looked alarmed but then as efficient as always. "Of *course* I will," she said with her customary grim efficiency when tasked with a responsibility.

Vivian hurried off and Myrtle hastily said, "We're really feeling just fine now, Tippy."

Miles added, "Never better."

"Nonsense. You're not putting me out whatsoever. We'll wait here until you're one-hundred percent again." Tippy gave them both an assessing look. "Did you go out into the heat?"

"We did," said Myrtle, straightening and trying her best to look extremely healthy and well. "I'm sure it was just the fact it was so humid out there that gave us a turn. But we've drunk water and are just fine. Aren't we, Miles?"

Miles immediately nodded. "Absolutely."

Tippy was never one to relinquish an assigned task. She knit her brows. "I'll get you some more water." She looked at the paper cups. "The water in these wasn't iced, was it?"

"It was definitely cool," said Myrtle.

Tippy pressed her lips together. "I'll just run down to the kitchen and get some ice water for you both. I can stay with you while you drink it."

She hurried away.

Myrtle said, "Let's go, Miles. If we hurry, we can drive away before she comes back from the kitchen."

Miles unhappily shook his head. "That wouldn't be very polite, Myrtle. Besides, she's concerned enough about our 'episode' that she might call Red to follow-up."

"You're always so ridiculously gentlemanly. She'd probably just think we had to find the restroom again."

Miles looked even more unhappy. "We haven't had to find the restroom even once."

"Well, if she comes back and makes us sit and drink that water, we'll certainly have to. And she's going to try to make you become a Methodist. And ride the church bus!" It was all too much for Myrtle. She stood up, steadying herself with her cane. "Let's get out of here."

But Tippy, who was a lot quicker than Myrtle gave her credit for, strode into the parlor with a small tray of waters and saltine crackers. As always, she was the perfect hostess.

"Stretching your legs, Myrtle?" Tippy asked briskly. "You're not getting stiff, are you? Why don't you change chairs? That might help. Oh, and I took the liberty of telling Dr. Fields about the two of you. He's on his way to check in."

Tippy was really taking her assignment entirely too seriously. Myrtle and Miles exchanged a grim look. There seemed to be no escaping this time.

So they sat there and drank down the cold water. Miles was shooting Myrtle daggers with his eyes. He was now doing two things he'd had no intention of doing—attending Myrtle's church and getting examined by a doctor.

Dr. Fields, apparently alarmed by Tippy, hurried into the room. He was an owlish man with thick eyeglasses. He gave Myrtle and Miles a sober look. "How are we doing in here?"

Myrtle said brightly, "So much better. I think Tippy's magical ice water has revived us. Don't you think so, Miles?"

Miles quickly nodded. "I feel great."

"Me too," said Myrtle. "Never better, as a matter of fact. We hate taking up your time, Dr. Fields. But I think Miles and I will just be on our way now."

The doctor looked relieved at being excused from his impromptu examination in the church parlor. "If you're sure. But Tippy and I will escort you to your vehicle. It's always good to be safe rather than sorry."

So they all trudged together to Miles's car. The unfortunate thing was that between the church service (despite all the hymns) and the enforced rest in the parlor, Myrtle was now rather stiff. She tried to cover it up as best she could by leaning heavily on her cane. Tippy, however, was eagle-eyed and noticed, a small line appearing between her immaculately-groomed eyebrows.

The good doctor and Tippy tucked them into Miles's car. Dr. Fields plied them with advice involving rest and hydration with electrolytes. Then they were sent on their way.

Miles said grimly, "I'm completely exhausted after all that. It's very tough to keep up a false pretense for that long."

"What? Oh, you mean about our joint medical episode." Myrtle shrugged. "It's not really that hard, Miles. Everyone expects people our age to be rife with health conditions. It's easy enough to play on their bias."

"Just the same, I think I'm ready for a nap," muttered Miles.

"At least we had the chance to speak with Vivian. I thought that was particularly enlightening, didn't you?"

Miles considered this. "I'm not sure it was. What did you find so interesting about our conversation?"

"The fact she blamed Dinah for Luther's death. The arguments she witnessed between Dinah and Luther must have been doozies. After all Dinah has done for Vivian to set her up on her feet again, it surprises me that she'd implicate Dinah like that."

Miles pulled into Myrtle's driveway. "Well, that probably has more to do with the fact that spouses are the most-likely suspects, don't you think? I can't really picture Dinah as a cold-blooded killer."

"Can't you? I think I can. It's not as if it was a messy or gruesome crime. Merely a poisonous pie."

Miles said, "Yes, but Dinah seems very upset by Luther's death."

"Not *really*. She's not upset by the fact she's lost Luther—she's upset by the fact that it happened in her house and she's not used to being alone. That's why she's having such a hard time sleeping. I don't think she's sitting around moping and missing Luther. He wasn't kind to her and he was generally disliked around town."

Myrtle turned to look at Miles. "What's on your agenda the rest of the day? Besides the nap?"

Miles sighed. "I really need to do some practicing for the chess tournament. It's tomorrow, you know. I have the horrible feeling Elaine is going to get in contact with me, too."

Myrtle shook her head. "I told you—she's playing the computer now. She should be leaving you completely alone."

"It's been such a busy day that I haven't even had the chance to fill you in. Elaine called me a little while ago. She keeps losing to the computer, even on novice, and can't figure out what she's doing wrong."

Myrtle said sadly, "I could tell her what she's doing wrong. Trying a new hobby. They so rarely go well."

"True. But she thinks I can diagnose the reason why she keeps losing. And I strongly suspect the reason she keeps losing is because she's bad at chess."

"Precisely," said Myrtle. "Just make sure she's set the level on the chess game to the easiest one possible. Maybe she's set it at a harder level than she thought she did."

Miles gave her a morose look. "I have the feeling that it *is* set on the easiest level. Anyway, visiting with Elaine is a possibility later. She mentioned that she'll need to come over after Red is back home so that he can keep an eye on Jack for her. So I guess it might be around suppertime."

"Or later," said Myrtle, raising an eyebrow. "Considering he's trying to track down a couple of murderers. Or at least one. Unfortunately, I told Wanda that I'd encourage Elaine's hobby, so I can't really say anything to her about trying to find something a bit more appropriate." She paused and then said, "Thinking about chess again. I was planning on coming to the tournament tomorrow, you know. I'm going to bring food."

"I don't think that's necessary," said Miles quickly.

"Of course it is! I looked on the tournament website and it explicitly mentioned that it would be wonderful if attendees brought food to share. I thought I'd prepare an elaborate snack. I've been on this website that has tons of recipes and ideas for snacks. Some of them are so clever. It made me feel quite inspired."

Miles looked wary. "Simple snacks are the best kind."

"What? That doesn't even make any sense, Miles."

"Yes, it does. If something is too elaborate, no one will want to mess it up. You wouldn't want to spend time on a snack that no one wants to eat."

Myrtle frowned. "Well, that's true. I guess I could end up producing something so amazing that no one will want to destroy it."

The wrinkles in Miles's brow eased a bit and he nodded.

"What sort of snacks go well with chess?"

Miles quickly answered, "Party mix."

"You mean like Chex cereal and pretzels and peanuts? That sounds more like a football snack than a chess snack. I think something a little sweeter might be good. Like the pudding I made. That wasn't elaborate."

Miles looked very concerned again now. Pudding had been one of Myrtle's more-recent disasters. "If you'd like to make something sweet, you could just put M&Ms in the party mix. Besides, football snacks are more like barbequed wings or nachos or sliders. Not party mix."

"Hm. I have the feeling you don't know very much about appropriate chess tournament snacks at all, Miles. Sugar will help everyone retain focus. It will give people energy. And it will keep the spectators from falling asleep. I'll bring a cookie pizza."

Miles gave her a wary look. "That sounds like a contradiction in terms."

"Not at all. It's a large cookie that you can cut into slices like a pizza. It will be perfect."

"You won't put tomato sauce on it, will you?" Miles seemed very concerned about this point.

"Of course not! Heavens, Miles, you're acting as if I might deliberately sabotage the snack I bring for the tournament."

Miles muttered something indecipherable under his breath. Then he said, "Okay. I'm going to go take that nap now."

"Enjoy," said Myrtle as she climbed out of his car.

Myrtle settled herself in the living room after making herself a cup of tea. It was the first hot drink she'd had in a while since it was so very hot outside. But today she felt like she wanted to spend some time thinking about Luther and Jasper's deaths. She thought about Dinah and the fact that she disliked desserts. The desserts made her think again about her cookie pizza. The cookie pizza thoughts made her realize she didn't have the ingredients in her house. Which made her come to the conclusion she needed a ride to the store. Miles, however, was taking a nap and she'd likely pestered him enough for the day, forcing him to church and making him have a medical issue.

Myrtle decided to call Elaine and see if she was available to go to the store.

Elaine, who always wanted to help if she could, sounded torn. "Oh, Myrtle. I could take you, but it would likely be the most stressful drive of your life."

Myrtle could hear the sounds of screaming coming from the background. "Are you and Red torturing my grandson?" she demanded.

"I think he's torturing us," said Elaine with a laugh that sounded more like a choked sob. "Red can drive you, though. I'm just about to start trying to cook dinner. I can pick you back up after you're done shopping, though. It's one of those fifteen-minute recipes."

The screaming seemed somehow more piercing than it had a moment before. "Can you even think with that din?"

Elaine said, "Oh, I'm going to put my headphones on. He's just tired and won't take a nap. He's eaten, he feels well—it's just the fact that he's nearly three."

Myrtle hadn't been nearly three for quite a long time and was increasingly glad that was the case.

Red took the phone from Elaine. "Mama? I'll be right there." He hung up.

Chapter Eighteen

Sure enough, Myrtle just had time to grab her purse and her cane and Red was at her door with his police cruiser running in her driveway.

"That was fast," she said.

Red answered dryly, "I was ready to get out of the house."

"What made poor Jack morph from a charming preschooler?"

Red said, "You know, Mama, there's really not very good cause and effect with that age group. It all seemed to start when he wanted to eat the crayons he was coloring with and I took them away from him."

"Seems rather illogical," said Myrtle with a frown. "But Jack is brilliant. Perhaps he was trying to indicate that he was hungry."

"He'd just had a snack," said Red. He glanced her way, "What are you picking up at the store?"

"I'm making a snack for the chess tournament tomorrow," said Myrtle in a complacent tone.

Red looked grim. "A snack? What—like party mix or something?"

"What is behind Miles and your obsession with party mix?"

Red chuckled. "So he suggested you make that too." He paused and then said persuasively, "It's because it's easy and tasty, Mama. Just cereal, nuts, and chocolate candy. It'll be a big hit at the tournament."

"Well, we'll never know because that's *not* what I'm making. I'm making a cookie pizza."

Red muttered, "That sounds ambitious."

Myrtle pressed her lips together in irritation. Then the mention of sweets made her think of something completely different, but related. "Isn't it odd that Dinah doesn't like sweets? I don't think I've run into many people who feel that way."

Red grunted noncommittally and pulled into the grocery store parking lot.

"Not many people actually know that Dinah doesn't like sweets. I've spoken to her about it."

"Of course you have." Red sighed.

"Are you absolutely positive that Dinah wasn't the target of the poisoned pie? Instead of Luther?" pushed Myrtle.

Red nodded. "Mama, Dinah doesn't have anybody at all who'd want her dead. Maybe her husband would have wanted to get her out of the way, but if so, he wouldn't have eaten the pie. Dinah Cobb doesn't seem to have an enemy in this world."

Red parked the car and started getting out to give Myrtle a hand out of the cruiser. She brushed him off and stood up. Then she scowled as he proceeded to escort her to the store.

"Thanks for the drive," she said pointedly. "Elaine said she could pick me up *after* I'm done shopping."

Red shook his head. "I'm in no hurry to return back home. Besides, I have a couple of things I need to pick up, myself."

"You have two murders to solve," reminded Myrtle.

"Yes. But I have to eat and sleep still. I *am* human."

Myrtle sniffed as if that fact was decidedly in question.

Red got a large cart, which made Myrtle sigh. She liked the smaller carts that she could maneuver around the aisles easier. Then he spent a long time in front of barbeque sauces.

"Maybe we should split up," said Myrtle. "It'll go faster that way."

Red snorted. "I did mention I'm not in a hurry to get home. It will probably take Jack about thirty minutes to settle himself down."

"Jack is clearly just over-tired," said Myrtle defensively. "Maybe you should go back and read him a story while poor Elaine cooks dinner."

Red looked a little guilty. "Maybe that's what I *should* do. But the fact of the matter is, I haven't had a whole lot of sleep since this investigation started. I'm not really at my best right now."

Myrtle decided that spending time with a Red that was not at his best was not exactly on her agenda. She grabbed one of the red baskets that the Piggly Wiggly grocery store had thoughtfully left at the end of various aisles. "I'll be back in a few."

Myrtle picked up a few things for her cookie pizza and was heading back to deposit them in Red's cart when she spotted Dinah Cobb picking up paper products in another aisle. "Dinah?" she called out.

Dinah turned and gave her a smile. "Miss Myrtle! How are you doing?" She frowned at the red basket Myrtle held. "Do you want to set that down in my cart? It looks sort of heavy."

"Oh, it's fine, thank you. I was just thinking about you, Dinah."

"Were you?" she asked. "That's sweet of you."

Myrtle realized she was going to be both very nosy and also fairly upsetting. She made sure her innocuous-old-lady demeanor was firmly in place. "I've just been worried about you. Your lack of sleep for one thing."

Dinah made a face. "That hasn't been much fun, I'll admit. Of course, you know a lot about that particular subject."

"Yes, but I don't seem to need as much sleep, so it's not as great of an impact. I was wondering if one of the reasons you can't sleep is because your subconscious is on alert." Myrtle peered at her with concern and glanced around to make sure Red was still preoccupied by the barbeque sauces and not heading in their direction.

"On alert?" repeated Dinah with concern. "You mean, I think I'm in danger? Or *am* in danger?"

Myrtle said slowly, "It's just that I was thinking it through. You don't like sweets but you mentioned the fact that no one really knows that except people who are very close to you. It seems to be that you might have been the target instead of Luther."

There was a crashing sound on the next aisle over that might have been canned goods hitting the floor. Myrtle winced. This conversation was going to be radically curtailed if Red happened over.

Dinah said, "Me? But I did ask Red that. He said it didn't appear that I gave anyone a motive." Her brow furrowed.

Myrtle gave her a reassuring smile. "I can't imagine anyone wanting to, Dinah. I'm just saying if you're not in the habit of locking your doors and keeping your windows shut, you might want to change your ways until Red finds who's responsible."

Dinah now looked extremely unsettled.

Red, as expected, came swiftly around the corner with his cart full of various sauces and mustards. Although he looked annoyed at Myrtle's conversation with Dinah, he didn't look as irritated as he should have been if he'd overheard Myrtle's exchange with her.

"Hi, Dinah," he said with a smile.

"Red," she said, nodding her head at him.

"Mama, I've gotten a call and need to head over to the station. Are you done shopping? I can drop you off by the house if you are."

Myrtle saw a way of both getting away from Red and continuing her talk with Dinah. "Not quite, no. And I'm trying to mentally recall some of the ingredients. It may take a little time. I'll just call Elaine when I'm done."

Red was in too much of a hurry to argue. "Okay. I'll just buy the stuff in my cart then. See you soon, Mama."

Dinah watched as Red bolted off for the checkout counter. "He must be so busy right now."

Myrtle shrugged. "I suppose so. Considering all the work he's doing, perhaps he'll figure out who the perpetrator is for these awful crimes." Changing tack swiftly, she said, "Back to you, though, Dinah. I was thinking that one way you might be able to stay distracted is by seeing someone new."

Dinah flushed a bit and looked away. But to Myrtle's eagle eyes, it didn't seem that Dinah was simply being shy or coy. It looked more like Dinah was actually already engaged in a relationship since she turned her face away so that Myrtle couldn't study it. "We'll see," Dinah said noncommittally. Then Dinah managed a rapid change of subject herself. "Isn't it terrible about Jasper? I keep thinking about that. He was alone, in the dark. He thought he was safe—but he wasn't." She looked morosely at the doors across the store. "And now it's even dark here. It's going to make me feel weird in the parking lot." She paused. "Myrtle, you're a friend of Ezra's aren't you?"

"Absolutely," said Myrtle stoutly.

"He was the one who found Jasper's body, wasn't he?"

"He did. And he called the police right away," said Myrtle. "Which was the responsible thing to do."

"It's sort of a coincidence, isn't it?" Dinah quickly lifted up a hand in defense. "Sorry, I know he's your friend. It's just—well, he has that poisonous plant in his greenhouse. And then he was the first one on the scene after Jasper is killed."

Myrtle said crisply, "Well, he wasn't the *first* one on the scene. That honor went to whoever murdered Jasper. Ezra was simply there to exercise. Besides, he didn't even know Jasper."

Dinah's eyebrows flew up. "But he did know Jasper. They were in high school together."

"They were in high school at the same *time*, yes. But that doesn't mean that they knew each other. Ezra hung out with a different crowd. I know because I taught him."

Dinah opened her mouth to argue but then stopped herself, probably not wanting to argue with an octogenarian in the middle of the Piggly Wiggly. Instead she said, "Goodness, I should be finishing up with these groceries and heading back. So good talking with you, Miss Myrtle."

Myrtle grunted a response. She was mulling over what Dinah had said. She'd had such conviction in her voice. She absently finished up her shopping, checked out her groceries, and then hesitated. She didn't like the doubt that Dinah had brought up in her mind. Best to just walk over to Ezra's place and ask him about it. He lived in easy walking distance of the store.

When she reached Ezra's house, she set down the bag of groceries and knocked firmly at the front door. He opened the door with a smile. "Miss Myrtle!"

Myrtle narrowed her eyes. "Ezra, did you know Jasper?"

Ezra swallowed and then stammered, "Know Jasper?"

"That's right. You said you didn't, but I just spoke with someone who had a different point of view." Myrtle's face was indignant.

Ezra slumped against the doorframe. "I didn't mean to lie to you. But I felt like a little misdirection might be in order. I used to be friends with Jasper in high school. I thought it was starting to look like I was too close to two murders."

"You two seem like very unlikely friends, Ezra. As I recall, Jasper was an athlete. You were always on the math team and in the horticulture club."

"Our paths ended up crossing because my dad wanted me to have some sort of involvement with high school sports. It didn't matter that I had absolutely no interest in it. He thought that was the only way for me to be a more-rounded person. I became the football manager."

"Football manager? I thought that was the coach's job," said Myrtle.

"It's a fancy name for a person who sets out the water coolers and the first aid station, collects dirty uniforms for the laundry—that kind of thing." Ezra shrugged. He looked at her groceries. "Would you like to come inside?"

Myrtle shook her head. "I don't have time to visit. But I do want to know, before I leave, what else you might be holding back. Do you know anything that might shed a little light on these two crimes?"

Ezra shifted uncomfortably. "I do know that Marshall and Luther had a terrible argument not long before Luther was murdered. Apparently, Marshall had witnessed Luther being hateful to Dinah and it made Marshall snap." He paused. "I just happened to be walking past Luther's and saw it when it happened. It reminded me what a hothead Marshall can be."

Myrtle frowned. This sounded remarkably like the excuse Jasper had used for visiting Luther the morning he found his body. But this time, the excuse rang true.

"Why didn't you bring this up earlier? It could prove to be an important lead. Maybe Marshall is the one behind these deaths."

Ezra sighed. "I didn't want to upset Lucinda. She's still crazily in love with Marshall and she'd be worried sick if she thought he might end up going to jail for murder. And an argument doesn't really mean anything—it's not actual evidence."

Myrtle said sternly, "It may not be evidence, but it can certainly point to a possible motive for murder. Maybe they ended up arguing again later and it got out of hand. You need to go to Red with this."

Ezra winced and Myrtle said, "I will, if you won't."

"Okay—I'll give him a call."

"Do that," said Myrtle. "Now I've got to head out and put these groceries away."

"You're *walking* back home?"

Myrtle shrugged. "I thought I'd have more stuff and I'd need to call Elaine, but I really don't seem to have many groceries."

Ezra got out his car keys.

Chapter Nineteen

Myrtle refrained from fussing on the quick trip back to her house. Instead, they spoke about safer topics—the unrelenting heat and Ezra's family and how they were doing. Ezra helped her bring her groceries in and then took off, likely with relief, into the night.

Myrtle now wanted to sit and think about all the things she'd learned about the case. Unfortunately, she felt she needed to go ahead and move forward with the pizza cookie. Or cookie pizza. She was never one to wait until the last minute to complete tasks and hated the thought of baking first thing in the morning when the tournament was that same day.

She started combining ingredients, still thinking about what she'd heard and seen. Dinah had seemed very flustered when Myrtle brought up dating. Was she *already* dating? And had she been even before Luther died?

Then she thought about Marshall and his argument with Luther. Why did Marshall care so much how Luther treated Dinah or how he spoke to her? Marshall certainly didn't strike Myrtle as that much of a gentleman. She was sure she'd seen him be curt with his wife, Lucinda. That made her think about Ezra covering up for Marshall, for Lucinda's sake since she was apparently still very much in love with her husband.

Myrtle looked down at the dough. It seemed like it was ready to go on the pizza pan. She brightened. Red and Elaine had given her a pizza pan for Christmas to help cook the various frozen pizzas she made. It was a fancy one, too, with holes in the bottom to evenly distribute the heat and keep the bottom from being soggy.

Myrtle smushed the dough with a spatula into the bottom of the pizza pan. Then she slid it into the preheated oven and set the timer for twenty-five minutes.

It had decidedly *not* been twenty-five minutes when the smoke detector started going off. Myrtle rushed into the kitchen to find that the cookie dough had melted, become runny, and dripped through the holes, splattering onto the bottom of the oven. Myrtle muttered imprecations under her breath as she opened the window and tried to shoo some of the clouds of smoke out of her house. The smoke detectors continued berating her for the mishap. She opened some windows on the front of the house, too. Then she set about removing the tray from the oven and throwing it into the sink.

There was a pounding on her front door. Myrtle sighed and walked over to answer it. Elaine was there, clutching Jack. You could tell by Jack's face that he'd very recently been ferocious but was now stunned to silence by the cacophony of smoke detectors.

"Myrtle!" gasped Elaine. "I thought I was picking you up at the store. And . . . is there a fire here?"

"False alarm," said Myrtle with a shrug.

"But there's smoke inside."

"Yes, but it's the kind of smoke that doesn't mean there's necessarily a fire."

Elaine's brow crinkled. "I thought the adage was 'where there's smoke, there's fire.'"

"Only sometimes," said Myrtle. "In this instance, it was just a case of cookie dough disagreeing with the fancy pizza pan."

"How did you get home?"

"Oh, Ezra drove me home from the store. I ran into him while I was out." Myrtle neglected to mention the fact that it was more of a seeking out than a run-in. She was never sure what information might find its way back to Red's ears.

Miles peered in Myrtle's front door with alarm. "Is everything all right here?" he shouted over the smoke detectors.

"Everything is lovely," said Myrtle dryly. "You're going to be so excited over the snack I've prepared for the chess tournament."

Miles visibly winced at the mention of chess.

Sure enough, Elaine quickly said, "Are we still on for tonight, Miles? Chess? After the day I've had, I can't wait to do something completely different from wrangling preschoolers. And I just can't figure out where I'm going wrong with these games."

Miles gave her a stricken smile.

The opened windows finally reduced the amount of smoke enough for the smoke detectors to shut off.

Elaine added with a laugh, "I won't be over too late. I can't stay up as late as you two do because I have to be up with the chickens with Jack."

Jack rubbed his eyes, already looking sleepy.

"As soon as Red gets back home, I'll run over for a little while."

Miles quickly said, "I'm not really sure exactly where I'll be."

"Oh, I can track you down. No worries."

On the contrary, however, Miles appeared to have quite a few worries.

Elaine left right as Jack set up howling again.

"Poor Jack," said Myrtle as she gently closed the door behind them.

"Poor Elaine," muttered Miles.

There was another tap on the door and Myrtle pulled it open again. "Forget something, Elaine?"

But it wasn't Elaine standing there. It was Erma grinning at her. Myrtle cursed herself for not looking through the window before opening the door.

"Isn't it so cozy here?" asked Erma unpleasantly, leering at Myrtle and Miles. "Sorry to interrupt you both. I thought I heard fire alarms going off." Her large nose sniffed the air. "And I definitely smell smoke."

"Everything is completely under control," said Myrtle coldly. "Although I thank you for your concern." She started to firmly close the door.

Erma, however, stuck her foot in the door to hold it open. "You know, it's important to replace the batteries in your smoke detectors."

"I think it's evident that my batteries are working."

Erma wagged her finger at her. "But now they've been running for a while. Might've worn the batteries down."

"She has a point," offered Miles.

Erma beamed at him. "Exactly. So you'll wanna replace them. Plus, Myrtle, I wanted to tell you something else I've found out. Since you're the hotshot detective, I thought you'd like a tip. But you better call me a sidekick!"

Myrtle's head began to throb between Erma's obnoxious voice and the former shrieking of the smoke detectors.

Erma continued, a smug look on her donkey-like features. "I know something about Marshall and Dinah."

It clicked together in Myrtle's head. To her horror, she realized Erma was right. Everything fell into place—Dinah's shyness when dating was mentioned. Marshall being so angry with Luther for his treatment of Dinah. But there was something more, too.

Before Myrtle could mull any further on it, Erma spat out, "Marshall and Dinah have been having an affair. I think it's been going on for *ages*. It's *shocking*, isn't it?"

It was, actually, a bit shocking. But there was part of Myrtle that felt Erma's big reveal was just confirming what she already knew on some level. "How do you know this?" asked Myrtle.

Erma said complacently, "I've now spotted them together two different times. The first time was before Luther died. I thought maybe Marshall had some sort of business with Luther, but Luther's car wasn't there at the time. He was probably at one of his many doctor appointments. Anyway, now I've seen them together *again* and they definitely looked like they were having a romantic interlude. They were *very* cozy." She gave them a hideous gaping grin.

Miles looked over at Myrtle and raised an eyebrow. She wanted to confer with her sidekick. Her *real* sidekick. To do so meant getting rid of Erma as quickly as possible.

Fortunately, it was right at that moment when Pasha came prancing in past Erma from the darkness outside into Myrtle's living room. The feral cat gave Erma a calculating look and then proceeded to use Erma as an impromptu scratching post.

Erma gave a bloodcurdling shriek and left Myrtle's house, slamming the front door shut behind her.

"Brilliant Pasha!" said Myrtle. "Somehow you always know exactly what to do."

Pasha purred up at Myrtle and lovingly brushed against her legs.

Miles carefully moved his legs out of the way in case Pasha wanted to use *him* as a scratching post.

Myrtle rubbed Pasha for a few minutes, cooing at her. Then she opened up a can of tuna—a generous treat for Pasha that she tried to reserve for special occasions since it was on the pricey side. Then she turned to Miles. "I think I'm having an epiphany."

"Aren't you supposed to scream 'eureka?'"

"Only if it's a scientific epiphany. This one doesn't qualify. I was just thinking about my conversation with Dinah and then Ezra. And even awful Erma's statement about Marshall and Dinah."

Miles tilted his head to one side. "Are you sure that's an epiphany? It sounds like a mess to me."

Myrtle said, "It makes absolute sense." She started to give him the rundown and then looked at the oven out of the corner of her eye. "This thing is a disaster."

It was indeed. There was burnt cookie pizza on the bottom of the oven in various degrees of ash. The air was still full of smoke. And the pizza pan was still caked with dough and in the sink. Myrtle put her hands on her hips and glared at the mess.

"A job for Puddin?" suggested Miles.

"I'm not sure even the new-and-improved Puddin will accept a mess of this magnitude." She scowled even more. "And the monstrosity will be made exponentially worse tomorrow if I don't clean it up because the dough will harden. I'd better just get this done now."

Miles said, "I'll give you a hand."

Myrtle picked the caked pan and Miles picked the oven. Myrtle said, "It's a pity this pizza pan is defective."

"Defective? I don't think I've ever heard of a defective pizza pan. I think a *pot* could be defective—maybe its handle isn't soldered on correctly. But a flat pan?"

Myrtle pursed her lips. "Then it's lucky you were an architect and not an engineer."

"I *was* an engineer," said Miles coldly.

"Well, the pizza pan has holes in it. Apparently, the dough gets greasy and slips right through the little holes to the oven floor."

"Myrtle, cookie dough is different from pizza dough. You can't expect the two things to behave the same way." He paused and then said, "I suppose this puts the kiss of death on your snack for the tournament tomorrow."

"If I didn't know better, I'd think you came in here and sabotaged my cookie pizza. You were always determined for me to bring party mix. And now I suppose I'm going to have to. I don't think I have enough of all of the ingredients to make another pizza." She gave the pan a particularly vicious scrubbing with her steel wool.

Miles gave a relieved sigh. Then he said, "What were you talking about? About your epiphany?"

"Yes. It was like a brainstorm, really. It all makes so much sense now."

Miles said, "You sound like one of those really annoying television detectives who knows the solution to the puzzle but doesn't give it away."

"I'm not trying to be enigmatic. I've just been very caught up with cleaning. The point of the whole thing is that *no one* was trying to kill Luther. Dinah was the target."

"What?" asked Miles. "But the police decided she wasn't."

The doorbell rang.

Miles started heading off into the back of Myrtle's house. "No more Erma for me," he muttered.

Myrtle knew from experience that it was fruitless to just not answer the door when Erma was outside, not when she knew you were at home. She would continue knocking at the door and ringing the bell. Then, she would simply assume that you'd suffered from some horrid medical malady (since Erma so often had them herself) and would call Red for a wellness check.

When she opened the door, though, it was Lucinda.

Chapter Twenty

Myrtle tried to close the door again and Lucinda shoved it open. "Miss Myrtle," she said, teeth gleaming. "Are you trying to keep me from visiting with you? I thought we were friends."

Myrtle gave her a sad look as she forced her way in. "I thought we were, too. But just friends through Ezra. I suppose you were the one who overheard my conversation with Dinah in the grocery store. The one who dropped the cans in the aisle next to me. I thought it had been Red, but he never said anything to me about it."

"That was a real stroke of luck," said Lucinda. "And then I saw you went right over to Ezra's. After he took you home, I had a visit with him, myself. Just a casual one, so he wouldn't suspect anything. I stayed long enough for him to recap your visit. He mentioned that I'd come up in conversation."

Lucinda pulled out a small pistol and Myrtle warily stepped backward. "It was hardly more than a stray remark. Ezra was simply saying how much you love Marshall. That was the only reason you came up at all." Myrtle's mouth was dry but she continued on, "That ended up being the crux of the whole case, though. You do love Marshall. And you blamed Dinah for taking him away from you."

"Because she *did* take him away from me. Marshall hasn't been the same toward me since."

Myrtle said, "The only thing I don't understand is why you would implicate Ezra like that. He's your best friend. Didn't you realize that it was going to look bad for him if you used the nightshade berries?"

"He was supposed to be still out of town at a conference, but came home a day early. I have a key to Ezra's house and I water his plants when he's out of town. I thought he was going to have an excellent alibi." Lucinda knitted her brows.

Myrtle said, "Look, I'm an old lady and I need to have a seat. I'm going to sit down at the kitchen table and we can talk there."

Lucinda brandished the weapon at her and Myrtle said coolly, "If you're waiting for me to put my hands up, it's not going to happen. I'm using a cane, as you know." She turned her back on Lucinda and headed for the kitchen. Lucinda wouldn't be able to see the rest of the house from the vantage point of the kitchen. Miles could come out from the back and either go for help or try to take on Lucinda, himself.

Unfortunately, Miles had decided to follow the second course of action. He hadn't fancied his chances of sneaking out the front door without getting shot on the way there. Miles stole stealthily out of the back of the house with the heaviest thing he could find—Myrtle's ancient iron. He slipped up behind Lucinda, lifting it menacingly.

Myrtle's house, however, was also not the newest; it had lots of creaky boards. Miles unerringly found the creakiest.

Lucinda was young enough to have much better reflexes than either Miles or Myrtle. She leaped up and said in a snarling voice, "Drop it."

Miles hesitated. Always one to follow directions, he said, "If I drop it, it might just bounce in the wrong direction."

"Put it *down*."

Miles carefully lowered the iron to the floor and rose with his hands up.

"Both of you back into the living room," said Lucinda, gesturing at them with the pistol. "I obviously can't trust either of you."

"That's a funny thing to say, considering the situation," said Myrtle with a sniff as she walked with Miles back to the living room. "It appears that *we* are the ones who shouldn't have trusted *you*."

Myrtle and Miles sat in the two armchairs and Lucinda perched across from them on the sofa, the pistol trained on them.

"I suppose you know how to use that gun. I do remember your father was quite a sportsman," said Myrtle.

Miles turned his head to look at Myrtle. She sounded very cool under pressure and her tone was conversational.

The de-escalation seemed to work, at least a little. Lucinda relaxed a bit. "Yes, he'd take me out shooting sometimes. We had some good times together."

"And Beverly? Your mom? How has she been? She was sick recently, wasn't she?"

Lucinda nodded. "She's better now. She had a bout of bronchitis and ended up with walking pneumonia."

Miles looked as if he wasn't quite sure how to react to Myrtle's impromptu chat with the person who clearly planned on doing away with them both.

He saw Myrtle glance from the clock back to Lucinda. "I haven't seen Beverly for a long while now. Is she still living at home with your dad?"

"No, they've both had to move to Greener Pastures. They couldn't keep up with the house anymore and I didn't have the time to help out as much as they needed me to." This small talk seemed to both calm Lucinda down and make her agitated all at the same time. She looked down at the gun in her hand as if half-wondering how it got there.

Which was exactly when the door flew open. Elaine said in a jaunty voice, "Chess anyone?"

There was no way Lucinda could cover both the front door and Myrtle and Miles simultaneously. She stood and spun around to point her pistol at the shocked Elaine. Myrtle handily stretched out with her cane and hooked Lucinda's leg, snagging it until she crashed to the floor with a cry. Miles scooped up the gun and, reflecting the military training Myrtle had forgotten he had, directed it steadily and expertly on Lucinda.

The next few minutes were rather chaotic. Myrtle backed up Miles by holding a fireplace poker in a very threatening manner while Elaine hurried back across the street to get Red and stay with Jack while Red came over. Which Red did, looking ferocious as he hurtled into the house, glaring at the vignette in front of him of Myrtle and Miles having to hold a killer at bay.

Red quickly put Lucinda in handcuffs, took the gun into evidence, and then greeted the state police, who arrived just minutes later.

Lucinda turned as she was led out the door to the waiting police car and said, "Sorry, Miss Myrtle." There was a genuine look of regret in her eyes.

Myrtle gave her a tight smile as Lucinda was escorted away.

Miles still looked slightly stunned by the turn of events.

"I think it's time for us to have a nice glass of sherry," said Myrtle. They walked into the kitchen and Myrtle poured them two sherries in her tiny crystal glasses. They sat down at her table, covered with its cheery red tablecloth.

"You could have knocked me over with a feather when I heard Lucinda threatening you," said Miles. "Did you know?"

"Well, I definitely suspected, which was what I was trying to communicate before everything went south. You see, Marshall was having an affair with Dinah."

Miles nodded. "Erma was clear on that."

"I started realizing Dinah Cobb was probably already involved with someone when I was talking with her at the Piggly Wiggly tonight."

Red, walking into the kitchen with Lt. Perkins, overheard the last bit. "Don't tell me that your hostage situation was caused by our trip to the grocery store tonight."

"As a matter of fact, it *was*, Red." Myrtle straightened in her chair a bit. "I *was* in a hostage situation, wasn't I?"

"Or a situation where you were about to be shot," said Red, sounding exhausted.

Perkins said, "What happened with Lucinda at the grocery store?"

"Well, I was having a conversation with Dinah Cobb while Red was perusing the barbeque sauces. I mentioned something about her dating again and got the distinct impression that she was *already* dating someone."

Red said wryly, "That hardly seems remarkable. Bradley could be a setting in a soap opera with all the dating and affairs going on."

"It wasn't that remarkable, no. But then I suggested that someone might have wanted to target Dinah, not Luther."

"That theory you broached in the car to me." Red rubbed his forehead. "So it apparently had some truth to it."

"Yes. And Lucinda was on the very next aisle over—I heard her dropping some cans, although I didn't realize it was her at the time. Dinah also casually mentioned that Ezra *did* know Jasper, which wasn't what he'd claimed. I ran by and visited him briefly, too."

Red groaned.

Lt. Perkins smiled at her. "It sounds like you were putting all the pieces together."

"My visit with Ezra really helped me with the final bits."

Red quirked a brow. "Because of his friendship with Jasper?"

"His friendship with Jasper had nothing to do with anything except it revealed that Ezra was more worried about being suspected of murder than he appeared. The main thing that came out of that visit, besides a ride home, was that Ezra said Lucinda was still very much in love with Marshall."

Red said, "You've lost me again."

"I think I'm following you," said Perkins thoughtfully. "Lucinda was jealous of Dinah's relationship with her husband. She decided to send her a poisoned pie."

Myrtle nodded. "Not realizing that Dinah wasn't a fan of desserts. Luther ended up eating it. Although I don't think Lucinda was very sorry that he did."

"An accidental death," said Red. He looked as if he very much might want to have some of Myrtle's sherry.

"And Jasper, I suppose, just got in the way," said Perkins.

Myrtle said, "Jasper was in the wrong place at the wrong time. He'd gone over to confront Luther again about reporting his son's vandalism. He saw Lucinda leaving the house. Maybe Lucinda was trying to get out of there quickly or maybe it looked like she had something to hide. He probably couldn't be sure that Lucinda was the one who delivered the pie that killed Luther—but he knew something wasn't right."

Perkins nodded. "Maybe he tried approaching her to give her a chance to explain herself. He'd have known Lucinda from school, I'm imagining."

"They were in the same grade with Ezra," said Myrtle. "But Lucinda ended up following along as he went on his early morning trip to the park for his usual workout."

Red threw his hands up in the air. "I thought she was such a fan of Ezra's! Why would she use nightshade berries as the murder weapon? It made it look as if he was involved."

"Lucinda was watering his plants while he was gone and had access to the greenhouse. Ezra was still supposed to be at a conference, but had come back a day early."

Perkins asked, "What made Lucinda decide to come over here? How did she know you were figuring it out?"

"Lucinda followed me from the store and saw me go into Ezra's house. After Ezra came back from driving me home, she paid him a quick visit. She somehow ended up with the impression that I'd gone over to Ezra's to ask him about her. Between that and what she'd overheard at the grocery store, she was sure I knew something. Sure enough to bring a gun with her, at least."

Perkins said, "Thankfully, you ended up all right."

"Thanks to Wanda," said Myrtle in a satisfied tone.

Red groaned again and Myrtle shot him a cross look.

"How did Wanda help out?" asked Perkins politely.

"She told me at the beginning of all this that I needed to encourage Elaine's interest in chess. And, bless her, Wanda was absolutely right. If Elaine hadn't run over here to have Miles help her out with her awful chess game, who knows what might have happened?"

Red stood up and gave another longing look at the sherries. "On that note Perkins, we'd probably better go have a talk with Lucinda." He turned again to his mother. "Mama . . . "

"You don't have to say it. I'm planning on just having a quiet evening and turning in."

"Good."

Perkins stood up too and smiled at Myrtle and Miles. "Thanks to both of you for your help with the case. You made some excellent deductions, Mrs. Clover."

She beamed at him. "Maybe now you can even make it to the chess tournament tomorrow."

Red said in an ominous tone, "Mama is baking a snack for it."

To his credit, Perkins maintained his smile.

"Actually, the cookie pizza suffered a mishap," said Myrtle carefully. "I'm planning on just picking up some party mix at the store."

"I'll see if I can make it over there tomorrow," said Perkins. "Thanks for thinking of me."

As Red and Perkins took their leave, Myrtle took a sip of her sherry. "You know what I need to do now?"

"Stay inside and turn in, like you were telling Red?" asked Miles.

"No. No, I need to call Dakota."

"Who? You mean the high school newspaper intern?"

Myrtle said, "Precisely. She should interview me for the article."

Miles smiled. "The one you're planning on having Sloan run on the front page?"

"It'll be an excellent story for her to use as a launching pad to get into a good college," said Myrtle in a satisfied tone. "And, of course, will be chockful of quotes from me. And you, too, Miles with your threatening iron and excellent firearm skills. I'll give her a call."

Dakota was delighted to write the story and her mother brought her right over. It turned out that Myrtle had taught Dakota's mother years ago. Dakota's mother, a middle-aged woman, proceeded to call Myrtle ma'am for the next hour. They ended up doing the interview back out on the dock where it was cooler since the oven disaster and the resulting open windows had led to Myrtle's house becoming quite warm. And while Myrtle and Miles recounted their harrowing story to an attentive Dakota, they all enjoyed ice cream by the lake.

About the Author

Elizabeth writes the Southern Quilting mysteries and Memphis Barbeque mysteries for Penguin Random House and the Myrtle Clover series for Midnight Ink and independently. She blogs at ElizabethSpannCraig.com/blog, named by Writer's Digest as one of the 101 Best Websites for Writers. Elizabeth makes her home in Matthews, North Carolina, with her husband. She's the mother of two.

Sign up for Elizabeth's free newsletter to stay updated on releases:

https://bit.ly/2xZUXqO

This and That

I love hearing from my readers. You can find me on Facebook as Elizabeth Spann Craig Author, on Twitter as elizabethscraig, on my website at elizabethspanncraig.com, and by email at elizabethspanncraig@gmail.com.

Thanks so much for reading my book...I appreciate it. If you enjoyed the story, would you please leave a short review on the site where you purchased it? Just a few words would be great. Not only do I feel encouraged reading them, but they also help other readers discover my books. Thank you!

Did you know my books are available in print and ebook formats? Most of the Myrtle Clover series is available in audio and some of the Southern Quilting mysteries are. Find the audiobooks here.

Please follow me on BookBub for my reading recommendations and release notifications.

I'd also like to thank some folks who helped me put this book together. Thanks to my cover designer, Karri Klawiter, for her awesome covers. Thanks to my editor, Judy Beatty for her help. Thanks to beta readers Amanda Arrieta, Rebecca Wahr, Cassie Kelley, and Dan Harris for all of their helpful suggestions and careful reading. Thanks to my ARC readers for helping to spread the word. Thanks, as always, to my family and readers.

Other Works by Elizabeth

Myrtle Clover Series in Order (be sure to look for the Myrtle series in audio, ebook, and print):

Pretty is as Pretty Dies

Progressive Dinner Deadly

A Dyeing Shame

A Body in the Backyard

Death at a Drop-In

A Body at Book Club

Death Pays a Visit

A Body at Bunco

Murder on Opening Night

Cruising for Murder

Cooking is Murder

A Body in the Trunk

Cleaning is Murder

Edit to Death

Hushed Up

A Body in the Attic

Murder on the Ballot

Death of a Suitor

A Dash of Murder
Death at a Diner (late 2022)
Southern Quilting Mysteries in Order:
Quilt or Innocence
Knot What it Seams
Quilt Trip
Shear Trouble
Tying the Knot
Patch of Trouble
Fall to Pieces
Rest in Pieces
On Pins and Needles
Fit to be Tied
Embroidering the Truth
Knot a Clue
Quilt-Ridden
Needled to Death
A Notion to Murder (2022)
The Village Library Mysteries in Order (Debuting 2019):
Checked Out
Overdue
Borrowed Time
Hush-Hush
Where There's a Will
Frictional Characters
Spine Tingling (late 2022)
Memphis Barbeque Mysteries in Order (Written as Riley Adams):

Delicious and Suspicious
Finger Lickin' Dead
Hickory Smoked Homicide
Rubbed Out
And a standalone "cozy zombie" novel: Race to Refuge,
written as Liz Craig